SOLVE YOUR OWN MYSTERY

THE MISSING MAGIC

STRIPES PUBLISHING LIMITED
An imprint of the Little Tiger Group
1 Coda Studios, 189 Munster Road,
London SW6 6AW

Imported into the EEA by Penguin Random House Ireland,
Morrison Chambers, 32 Nassau Street, Dublin D02 YH68

A paperback original
First published in Great Britain in 2022

ISBN: 978-1-78895-445-7

A CIP catalogue record for this book is available from the British Library.

Printed and bound in the UK.

The Forest Stewardship Council® (FSC®) is a global, not-for-profit organization dedicated to the promotion of responsible forest management worldwide. FSC defines standards based on agreed principles for responsible forest stewardship that are supported by environmental, social, and economic stakeholders. To learn more, visit www.fsc.org

2 4 6 8 10 9 7 5 3 1

SOLVE YOUR OWN MYSTERY

THE MISSING MAGIC

GARETH P. JONES
ILLUSTRATED BY LOUISE FORSHAW

LITTLE TIGER
LONDON

CLASSIFIEDS

MAGICON

The world's biggest REAL MAGIC convention comes to Haventry.

For saver tickets, ask for the ABRACA-DISCOUNT.

Join us in the ultimate war of good vs. evil!

All meetings include tea & cake.

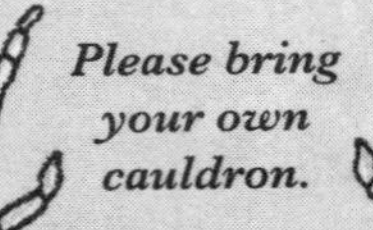

Please bring your own cauldron.

Get your whites whiter with our mummy laundering service.

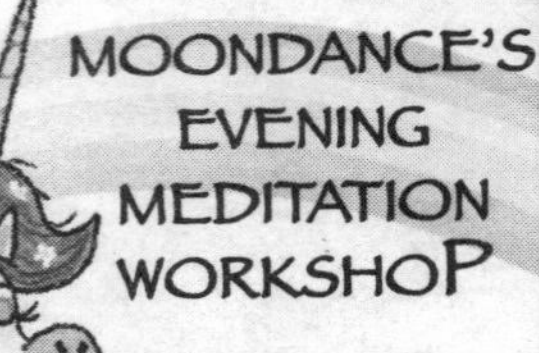

Turn up, tune in, drop out and 'channel your inner unicorn' with Moondance, the world's most inspirational unicorn guru.

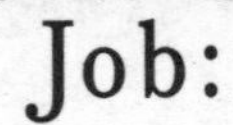

Job:

Private Investigator's Assistant

Long hours, low pay, hard work.

Based on the Shady Side of town!

NIGEL'S

ELFTRONICS EMPORIUM

Talking toasters, walking foot spas and more!

Put some sparkle into your life with our household items – all powered by clean, renewable magic.

MISSING
NO.1
~~ELF~~
ASSISTANT
MAGICON

DETECTIVE
EDWIN'S STUFF
MAGICON

NEWS OF THE UNUSUAL

YOU EASE THE OFFICE DOOR open and step inside as quietly as possible. You hope your boss won't notice how late you are, but the door slams shut behind you.

Klaus Solstaag is leaning back in his chair, resting his large, hairy feet on the desk. The breeze from three fans ruffles his fine white hair. It's chillier inside the room than on the street but, as Klaus always reminds you, yetis like the cold.

He grunts at you from behind a newspaper. "What time d'you call this?"

You explain that after setting off in plenty of time, you ran into a few problems on your journey across town. First, you were stuck waiting for a particularly long ghost train to rumble past. Then, you had to find a different route because a couple of burly Unusual Police Force officers had sealed off a road following a suspected gas leak around Haventry City Hall. And finally, you were caught in a bottleneck of witches and wizards queuing up to buy newt eyes and lizard tongues from a pop-up market stall.

"Don't worry about it. This is the busiest I've ever seen the Shady Side," says Klaus. "It's all because of this."

He holds up this morning's edition of the *News of the Unusual*.

MAGICON IS ON!

Haventry is preparing to welcome witches, wizards, warlocks, mages and magicians from all over the world as it plays host to the world's biggest real magic convention, Magicon.

Find out what's going on with our free pull-out event guide.

There was a time when you would have been checking the date to see if it was April Fool's Day but, since becoming a detective's sidekick on the Shady Side of Haventry, you've grown accustomed to a world full of weird and wonderful people and things. You glance out of the window where a water sprite is hovering with a bucket of water and a sponge, cleaning the window.

Klaus continues to read. "For the first time in over

a hundred years, Haventry will be the centre of all things magical as the world of wizardry descends upon it. There are events all over town, while the main guest panels, workshops and discussions take place in the Haventry Exhibition Centre." Klaus looks up from the paper and chuckles. "That's on your side of town, but all your lot will assume it's ordinary people dressed up as witches and wizards."

It always amazes you how most of Haventry's human population remain blissfully unaware of its more unusual Shady Side inhabitants. You've been working here for so long, this world of monsters and mythical creatures feels normal to you.

Klaus turns his attention back to the newspaper. "The biggest event of all will be the opening ceremony at ten p.m. tonight in Shady Side Stadium."

You glance up at the clock on the wall. It's midday. Ten hours to go.

"Night Mayor Franklefink is appearing at the ceremony personally, and UPF officers are on high alert as the city is flooded

by not just good wizards and witches but also the League of Evil, sworn devotees of Enid the Evil Enchantress, who are dedicated to seizing control of the w—"

POP!

The noise makes you jump. All three fans stop whizzing around. Klaus looks at you. "That's weird," he says. "I bought these fans from Nigel's Elftronics Emporium. They run on magic so a power cut shouldn't affect them."

"Excuse me, would you mind giving me a hand?" says a voice.

It takes you a moment to realize it's coming from outside. Klaus jumps up and opens the window. The water sprite is clinging on to the windowsill, his legs and spindly wings flailing.

With Klaus's help he climbs up and drops into the room. He's covered in soapy water. You stick your head out of the window to see that his bucket and sponge are now lying on the pavement.

"What happened?" asks Klaus.

"My wings have stopped working. It must have been a bad batch of fairy dust." The sprite flaps his wings as hard as he can but he remains on the floor.

He's not the only one to have suddenly lost his ability to fly. There is a large pile of moaning witches lying in the middle of the road. One is hanging from a telephone wire, with her broomstick in one hand, and her stripey legs below. A truck has swerved to avoid the witches and crashed into a bookshop. The owner of the shop is waggling his wand frantically at the broken window crying, "Toadstools and lizards, clouds and grass! A whish and whoosh and I'll repair this glass."

Nothing happens.

"Come on." Klaus spins around and grabs his hat and coat.

You follow him out of the office and down into the street. As soon as you step out the door, a young goblin slips on the soapy water from the sprite's bucket and goes flying. You dive out of the way.

The dangling witch lets go of the wire and drops on to a passing caravan. Her robes cover the windscreen, and the caravan crashes into a lamp post. A jet of steam shoots from the caravan's engine, then the witches Burnella and Bridget Milkbird stagger out, coughing and spluttering.

A wizard runs past screaming, "The end is nigh. All is lost. My wiz is a was!"

"His wiz never was much of a wiz, even when it was a wiz," says Burnella.

"Er, what?" asks Klaus. "What's going on?"

"The magic has vanished," replies Burnella.

"Really?" says Bridget. She waves her wand at you and yells, "Azaka-bam, Azaka-burm, make this human a wiggly worm!"

You cower in fear then open your eyes and look down, terrified of what you might see. To your relief, all your limbs remain intact. You are not a worm. You are still you.

"Oh no. The magic really *has* gone," wails Bridget. She looks at her sister. "But how are we going to make the po—"

Burnella nudges her sister and interrupts. "Potatoes. Yes, you're right. We're supposed to be catering for Magicon this weekend and we magic folk do like our spuds. We won't cope with all the orders without magic."

A scruffy witch with twigs in her hair runs straight into you.

"Oh, fudgenuts and pumpkin juice, the magic's gone! What are we to do?"

There are signs of chaos all around. The witches who just fell from the sky pick themselves up and try to take off again, leaping up from the pavement, only to find themselves collapsed in the gutter. The wizard with the smashed window keeps shouting the same spell over and over. These people don't know what to do without magic.

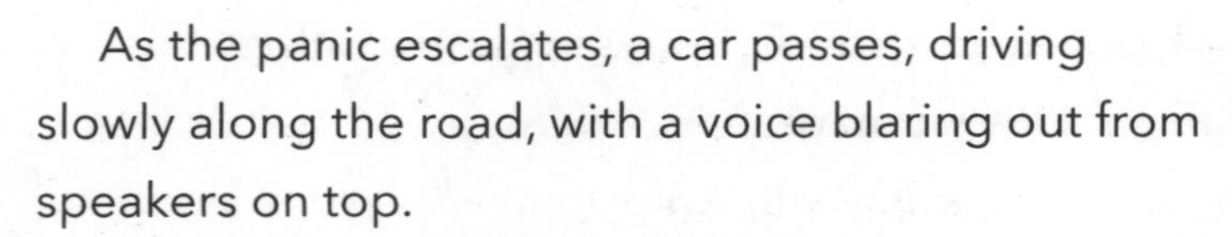

As the panic escalates, a car passes, driving slowly along the road, with a voice blaring out from speakers on top.

"Shady Side citizens … please remain calm. There is a temporary glitch with the abraca-router but rest assured, we have our best people working on it and the magic will be working again soon."

The car stops to avoid running over the confused gaggle of witches, and in the passenger seat you spot the monster-making scientist Night Mayor Franklefink holding a microphone to his mouth, making the announcement.

"Typical politician, just saying what people want

to hear rather than the truth," says Burnella. "The abraca-router *can't* glitch. The only way this could happen is if the magic has been stolen!"

"How can you steal magic?" asks Klaus.

"It's not so hard for an experienced magic-wielder," replies Burnella.

"I blame Grand Master Dimbleby for this," snaps Bridget. "As Head of the Magic Circle, the magic of this town is his responsibility. No one would have dared steal it if Enid was in charge."

"Ha, you have such a witch-crush on Enid the Evil Enchantress," says Burnella, with a dismissive wave of her hand.

"I do not," says Bridget.

Burnella bends down and speaks quietly in your ear, "She's got a poster of Enid in her bedroom. She talks to it sometimes."

"What are you muttering about?" demands Bridget. "There'll be no muttering once Enid has struck the first blow in the ultimate war of evil against good."

"Ultimate war indeed." Burnella shakes her head and smirks. "My sister is all talk. Every Magicon, the League of Evil has a vote on whether they should rise up and destroy the world and, every time, they vote against it because, well, to be honest, it's a bit of a faff, isn't it?"

"This time will be different," says Bridget.

"Why?" asks her sister.

"Never you mind, but you'll see. I'm so excited Enid is here, I could burst. Look at her!" Bridget whips out a large book – *The League of Evil Annual*. On the front cover is a picture of a witch with long black hair that falls across her face like a shadow. Underneath is written, *THE WITCH IS BACK!* Something about the picture sends a chill down your spine.

"Evil Enid," says Klaus. "Is she the one who created that plague of bloodsucking rodents?"

Bridget nods enthusiastically. "VampiRats! Yes, some of her greatest work."

"A power-hungry witch who relishes chaos and evil," says Klaus. "Yes, it does sound like the case of the missing magic might be closed before it was even opened."

"I don't think Enid took the magic," says Burnella. "Remember evil witches and wizards need magic as much as good ones."

She pauses and you hear Franklefink repeating his message.

"… please remain calm. There is a temporary glitch …"

"Just listen to him, spinning lies and making himself the centre of attention as usual," says Burnella.

You've encountered Franklefink in the past. He was a slippery enough character before he became a politician. Now he runs this town, there's no knowing what secrets he might hold.

Klaus turns to you. "I think you should be writing this—" He sees that you already have your notepad open. You understand that even though no one has hired you, the town needs your help, which means you have a case to solve. In bold letters at the top of the page you write, *The Missing Magic*. Underneath, you write *Enid* and *Franklefink* although it's too early to say if either of them are suspects.

"So where would we find this precious leader of yours?" asks Klaus.

"Yeah, good luck with that," says Bridget. "Enid can transform into any shape she wants. She was doing her giant spider at this morning's evil coffee morning, but she scuttled off straight after that. Who knows what form she's taken now."

"You're right. If she has all this magic at her disposal, she's going to be hard to track down," says Klaus.

You continue making notes. It makes sense that your prime suspect would be a self-proclaimed evil witch bent on an ultimate war but, as Klaus has told you many times, the obvious answer is rarely the right one. It's what you love about your job. You're considering possibilities when a huge, grey-skinned head in a chef's hat appears from the caravan. It belongs to Bootsy, the witches' monster.

"Cooker no cook," he says.

"Of course the cooker's not working. It runs on magic. So does pretty much everything around here," says Burnella. "I told you we should have gone electric this time instead of relying on Nigel's Elftronics."

Klaus turns to you. "It might be worth interviewing Nigel Rigmarole about this," he says. "After all, magical energy is his business."

You write down *Nigel Rigmarole* and *Elftronics*.

"What about the scene of the crime?" says Klaus.

"That would be the abraca-router in the Magic Circle's headquarters," says Burnella.

"Er, I wouldn't go down there," says Bridget. "With the magic gone there's nothing to stop Bet—"

"Shh!" whispers Burnella.

"What?" asks Klaus.

"Nothing," say both witches.

"Or maybe I should just keep an eye on you two," says Klaus. "Because I'm getting the impression there's something you haven't told us."

You have the same feeling.

"Watch us all you like, but we're not going anywhere," says Bridget. "Not until we get a mechanic for Susan."

The caravan shudders.

"Susan hates a trip to the mechanics because they always scrape the rust off her bottom," says Burnella.

"It's her own fault for turning herself into a caravan in the first place," adds Bridget.

"Not to mention turning my dog into a car," says Klaus. "Talking of which, where is Watson?"

He sticks his fingers in his mouth and whistles. You hear the barking rev of an engine as Watson appears round a corner. He pauses to cock his rear wheel and send a squirt of oil up the side of the witches' caravan. You slide into the passenger seat, while Klaus grabs the steering wheel. Just ahead, you spot Franklefink's car heading out of sight.

"... rest assured, we have our best people working on it and the magic will be up and running again soon," says the voice through the speaker.

"So where should we start?" asks Klaus. "Shall we see if we can check out this abraca-router first?"

? Do you want to start with the abraca-router?

Turn to page 49

BARKING UP THE RIGHT TREE

? Or would you rather speak to Franklefink?

Turn to page 37

DRIVE-THROUGH NIGHT MAYOR

A Familiar Monkey

FOLLY HEIGHTS IS ONE OF the oldest buildings in Haventry. A tall, cylindrical stone tower, it casts a long shadow over the Shady Side. Before you started working with Klaus, you always believed that the tower was empty. In truth, Folly Heights contains some of the most exclusive rented rooms in the city and plays host to only the wealthiest visitors. On the outside various signs warn:

UNSOUND STRUCTURE

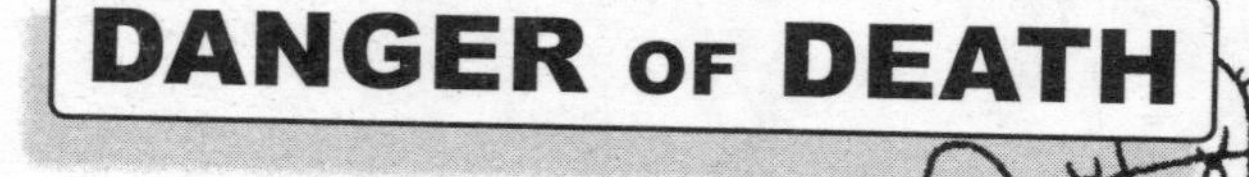

Klaus pushes aside a roll of barbed wire and opens a door in the central spire. As you enter, the sound of each footstep bounces off the walls, as loud as gunshots. A winding staircase curls around the inside of the tower. There is no handrail. It's a long way up but an even longer way down.

"Even if your average Joe did stumble in here, there's no way they would risk going up," says Klaus.

In spite of your reservations, you push yourself against the wall and follow him, but the spiral stairs make you feel dizzy and breathless. They seem to go on forever but eventually you reach a door at the top.

Klaus knocks.

"One moment, please," says a voice.

When the door opens you find yourself staring at a monkey wearing a waistcoat and top hat. He leans on a black walking stick with a silver top.

"We're not interested, thank you," he says, trying to close the door again.

Klaus puts out a large, hairy foot to keep the door open. The monkey looks down at it and tuts.

"Do you mind?" he says. "We're rather busy."

"We?" says Klaus. "Which *we* would that be, then? And while we're at it, who are you?"

"My name is Mr Charles Evans," says the monkey.

"Devoted follower, apprentice and familiar to Enid the Evil Enchantress. And who, pray, are you?"

"Klaus Solstaag, private detective, and this is my assistant." He pats you on the back.

The monkey looks at you as though he hasn't noticed you before. His eyes are unnerving. You've seen a lot of strange things while working for Klaus, but there's something especially odd about this alarmingly human monkey.

"We don't need any investigating at the moment, thank you very much."

Once again, Evans tries and fails to close the door.

"Sorry. I have a few questions for your mistress," Klaus says.

"We don't really use that term. I serve her and do her evil bidding and all that, but I'm still my own man."

"Or your own monkey?" suggests Klaus.

The monkey glances down at himself as though surprised to see his body. "Yes, of course." He laughs. "I sometimes forget."

"You weren't always a monkey, then?" says Klaus.

"Funny story about that." He shows you his palms. "These were once the hands of a man, before I had the great fortune of being turned into a monkey whose only duty is to serve the enchantress."

"Er, so you wanted to be a monkey?" asks Klaus.

"I didn't know I wanted to be a monkey until I was a monkey." He smiles. "Now I am a monkey, I wouldn't have it any other way. Enid is such an inspiration. I once witnessed her make a volcano erupt. You should have heard the screams from the villagers. It was exquisite. I do love to watch her work."

"Er ..." Klaus turns to you, signalling with his eyes that there's something not quite right about this monkey.

"Why did she choose you as a familiar?" asks Klaus.

"Well ..." He looks down at his feet and shuffles, embarrassed. "I was a witch hunter, you see. Enid was my nemesis. Back then, before my eyes were opened, she would do evil and I'd do my best to thwart her. I did a lot of good thwarting too. Then, one dark and stormy night, she caught me in her castle, turned me into a monkey and I've been her familiar ever since."

"I thought a familiar was supposed to be loyal."

"Oh, I am, sir. Loyal as they come. There's nothing

I wouldn't do for Enid. It turns out doing evil is much more fun than thwarting it."

"I see," says Klaus. "So you changed, then?"

"Yes. Into a monkey, sir. Aren't you listening? Isn't he listening? Which one of you should I be addressing?"

The monkey looks at you but Klaus is quick to respond. "You can stick with me for the moment. Maybe if I could come in and get a glass a water. Those were a lot of stairs."

"I'm afraid that's not possible. This place is a mess and Enid is most particular about how she presents herself in public. For many witches and warlocks, she's a role model."

He tightens his grip on the door. He really doesn't want you to see inside.

"Then perhaps you could fetch Enid," says Klaus.

"I would if I could, sir. I *would* if I could. But she's not here, see."

"Where is she?"

"That is a very good question. It's one I have been pondering myself. We had one of our coffee mornings first thing today. The League of Evil do love a good coffee morning. Enid did her thing - you know, promised to take over the world and smite all those who stand in our way, then we brought out the biscuits. It was all perfectly normal and evil, but I haven't seen her since."

"Is it unusual for her to vanish like that?" asks Klaus.

"Not especially. You know what evil witches are like. They're mysterious and malignant by nature. She'll turn up. She'd better. We've got a secret meeting this afternoon and a drinks reception this evening before the opening ceremony."

As the monkey talks to Klaus, you subtly lean to the side to see into the apartment. With white walls and very little furniture there isn't much of interest, but you do notice that a window is open and a curtain is flapping. The bottom of the curtain is blackened and singed.

"So Enid hasn't been seen since before the magic vanished?" asks Klaus.

"That's right. I only hope they get it back on as soon as possible. Enid likes to put on a show for her fans. They adore her, of course."

"Of course," says Klaus. "She's a power-hungry witch-queen of evil. What's not to love?"

"Precisely," says Mr Evans, apparently oblivious to the sarcasm in your boss's voice.

"Some people are saying she might be responsible for the magic going missing in the first place," says Klaus.

The expression that crosses the monkey's face suggests that the thought never occurred to him. "I'm not saying it's impossible that an evil enchantress intent on world domination would do such a thing but if you want the humble opinion of this monkey, I suspect someone wants us to think it was her."

"You reckon she's being set up?"

"We evildoers are often the scapegoats for things like this. And it's well known that we have a big vote coming up. If we win this one, we'll be on the road to ultimate victory."

"I can see why some people might object to that," says Klaus.

"Yes, the establishment will go to any lengths to stop us disrupting their cushy lives."

"And when you say the establishment, you mean ..."

"Oh, you know. People like Franklefink and his team of busybodies at Haventry City Council," replies Mr Evans. "They're all as bad as each other, but not bad in a good way, if you know what I mean. Bad in a bad way. Night Mayor Franklefink is a total nightmare. The only one with any sense on the council is Sandra Rigmarole, the District Governor. I have to say, despite being one of them, she's actually done a good job organizing Magicon. If you want to find out what's really going on in this town, you should talk to her rather than bothering me."

This isn't the first time the surname Rigmarole has come up in this investigation and you know that all elves have the ability to use magic.

"But instead," Evans continues, "you come here because you're just like everyone else, accusing Enid without a shred of evidence. Meanwhile, Moondance is parading around showing off that he's still got magic. If that's not suspicious, I don't know what is."

"Who's Moondance?"

"He's a unicorn in town for Magicon, but you wouldn't dream of accusing him, would you? Oh no. He's all about peace and love. It's always the evil ones who get accused."

"Interesting." Klaus glances at you, ensuring that you write the name in your book. "Where would we find this Moondance?"

"Here." Mr Evans hands you a leaflet.

MOONDANCE MEDITATION
JOIN THE WORLD'S LEADING LIGHT IN RELAXATION TO DISCOVER
YOUR INNER UNICORN.
ROOM 24, HAVENTRY EXHIBITION CENTRE

"Thank you." Klaus removes his foot from the door and Mr Evans slams it shut.

"That monkey gave us a couple of names, but maybe he was just trying to distract us from searching for Enid," says Klaus. "Still, I do wonder if we should try to catch up with this unicorn before his next session starts. Or, if you think Sandra Rigmarole is worth talking to, then we should head to the City Chamber."

? Do you want to visit Sandra Rigmarole?

Turn to page 76
THE 99TH FLOOR

? Or do you want to find Moondance the unicorn?

Turn to page 60
MOONDANCE THE RADIANT

"FRANKLEFINK HAS MANAGED TO UPSET pretty much every member of the Shady Side community since he became Night Mayor," says Klaus. "He's limited how much vampires can withdraw from blood banks. He's increased the price of brains so the zombies are moaning about that. He's introduced a pointy-ears tax, which has upset the elves. And he's saying the mermaids have to use their own toilets from now on. I can't see him being voted in again at the next election at this rate."

Franklefink's car turns into a busy road just as a giant steps on to a pedestrian crossing in front of you. Klaus slams on the brakes and you feel the jolt of the seat belt.

"Don't worry," says Klaus. "Watson has got his scent now. Haven't you, boy?"

Watson revs his engine in response then lurches backwards. He skids and steers skilfully around the enormous foot. He takes the corner so fast, you're pushed up against the window. He dodges in and out of traffic as he tries to catch up with Franklefink's car. Your knuckles whiten as you grip the seat. On the way, Watson mounts the pavement, veers all over the place and jumps red lights. People cry out in fear.

There's a sudden jolt as the car drops off a pavement into a drain and causes your hand to knock the radio on. Watson is always tuned in to Shady Side Radio. The DJ is saying, "Here to discuss the news is roving reporter Gretchen Barfly-Sewer ..."

"Hello." The rasping voice belongs to a banshee reporter you have encountered on previous cases. A high-pitched laugh makes you grit your teeth. You pinch yourself and focus on the pain in an effort to keep your head clear and unaffected by the persuasive power of banshee laughter.

"So, Gretchen," says the reporter. "Any idea how this awful accident could have happened?"

"Accident? This is no accident, despite what that old fraud Franklefink would have you believe. Any experienced magic-wielder will tell you it's theft – pure and simple."

"If this is about gaining ultimate power then surely it can't be a coincidence that the Enchantress Enid is in town to rally her League of Evil," says the DJ.

"Yes, and just imagine what she could do with all that power," says Gretchen.

"I assume you'll be following this story throughout the day in the *News of the Unusual*?" asks the DJ.

"I would but the printing press is magic, isn't it?"

replies Gretchen tetchily. "We can't print a thing. But if I could get the paper out, I would be reminding my readers that this happened on Dimbleby's watch. As Head of the Magic Circle he should take full—"

Klaus turns off the radio. "Right, it looks like Franklefink is picking up some grub, so let's see what he knows. As Night Mayor he should have all the latest information. Though whether he's willing to share it with us is another question."

Watson comes to a standstill behind Franklefink's car in a drive-through fast food restaurant called Zombie Bites, with a menu that includes Brainy Burgers, Monster Nibbles and Mummy Wraps. Another poster proudly proclaims:

All-You-Can-Eat
Apocalypse Tuesdays
It's the end of the world – and your diet.

You gulp when you see the picture of a leering zombie, mouth smeared in what you hope is tomato ketchup. Night Mayor Franklefink steps out of the car and walks over to make his order. He wears a white lab coat and a heavy gold chain around his neck. It clangs against the speaker.

"A big Zomboy Burger Meal with large Creepy Cola, please," he says.

A terrifying groan comes from the crackly speaker, followed by an eerie silence. Here on the Shady Side, even ordering fast food can be a scary experience. You and Klaus step out of the car. As you approach, you notice that Franklefink's driver appears to be a large, blubbery seal, wearing a smart black cap.

"Ah, Night Mayor Franklefink," says Klaus. "I'm glad you're finding time to eat during this crisis."

"Crisis, Klaus? What crisis?" Franklefink smiles, then says to his driver, "Julian, take the car around to the pick-up point while I have a quick chat with these highly valued voters."

"Aye, sir," says the seal-man, lifting the handbrake and moving the car.

"Julian's a first-rate assistant. He certainly gets my seal of approval." Franklefink laughs at his own joke then adds, "And that's quite a thing – after all, I am the most important person in Haventry these days."

"Even if you do say so yourself," says Klaus. "So, the magic has been stolen. What are you doing to find it?"

"Actually, we're downplaying the theft angle of this situation," says Franklefink. "We're calling this a *momentary inconvenience*. We don't want to cause any more upset than necessary. There really is nothing to worry about. It will be back on again in no time."

You stumble and lurch to the side as the ground unexpectedly shakes.

"What was *that*?" asks Klaus.

"Oh, just a minor tremor caused by one of those goblin mining crews. It's a problem that I am currently dealing with by introducing measures that would ban goblins from Haventry altogether. It's just one of the ways I intend to restore proper order to our community."

"I'm not here to listen to speeches," says Klaus.

"Yes, well, the full speech will be delivered this evening at the opening ceremony where I shall reveal to the world my plans to revolutionize this town, as well as unveiling my latest creation! The real crime would be to miss that."

"You've made another monster?"

A grin spreads across his face. "No longer will they dismiss me for only having made one measly monster."

"That's no way to talk about your own son," says Klaus. "Monty's a good kid."

Franklefink waves a hand dismissively. "Oh, he's fine, but he is a mere shadow compared to my new venture. When everyone gathers this evening, you will all bear witness to the birth of a new age of monsters!"

Klaus smiles. "Doesn't all this depend on the magic being back in time?"

"Yes, yes, of course. The Monster Maker runs on magic. It's vital to my plan that the magic is back on for my big announcement, but I have faith that it will be by then," says Franklefink. "But you don't need to worry about any of this. The UPF have the matter under control. Leave it to the professionals, Klaus."

Klaus raises his eyebrow. As he always tells you, if anyone puts an obstacle in your way, it's because there's something they don't want you to find out. You know from previous experience that Franklefink is a man with secrets, and you wonder if he knows more about the missing magic than he's letting on. He seems very certain it will be restored before the ceremony.

"Your order is now ready for collection. Next customer, please," groans the voice from the speaker.

"Oh, right. Well, it would be rude not to order something," says Klaus.

It isn't the first time your boss has been distracted by his stomach. Being hungry is pretty much a permanent state for yetis as far as you can tell.

Night Mayor Franklefink goes to pick up his food. While Klaus reels off his usual favourites from the menu, you follow Franklefink. His selkie driver flops out of the door, waddles around the car and opens a door for Franklefink, who holds a paper bag full of junk food.

"Thank you, Julian," says Franklefink. "You can have five minutes' ball practice while I take a private call."

"Very good, sir."

Franklefink lobs out a stripey beach ball then slams the door shut. Julian catches the ball on his nose, and starts doing keepy-uppies with his nose, tail and flippers. It's entertaining to watch but you know you mustn't get distracted. With Night Mayor Franklefink on his call and Julian busy with his ball, you decide to take a look in the back of the car.

An enormous body lies on the back seat, covered by a white sheet. A name tag hangs from the large toe: *Enormelda*. You've seen this lifeless monster before. Franklefink wanted to bring her to life the last time you met him. He must be planning to finally do so at the opening ceremony. The car is also stacked with smaller white boxes. On top of them is something that looks a bit like an old-fashioned sewing machine that you recognize as the Monster Maker. An attached label reads,

DUH-DUH-DUUUUH!

Dramatic organ music plays. It takes you a moment to realize that it's the sound of Franklefink's phone ringing.

"Hello." His voice is muffled. You press your ear against the back window. "Yes. Ah, Detective Inspector Rigmarole. So, regarding Enid, my sources tell me that she's rented a room at Folly Heights … Oh, also, please could you look into—"

HOOOOONNNKKK!

You press your hand against your other ear to block out the sound of Julian happily honking to himself.

"—investigate … I don't care. While I'm in charge, you'll do as I say. I'll—"

HONK-HONK-HONK!

Julian is now performing a series of backflips, while keeping the ball in the air.

"—at the press conference this afternoon."

Franklefink hangs up and beeps the horn. Julian catches the ball in his flippers and returns to the car. You quickly move away, mulling over what you just heard. Since he became Night Mayor, Franklefink has shown he wants to control what the public know. It's different for you. You want to peel back everyone else's versions of events and unpick the truth.

You return to Klaus, who has an even bigger paper bag full of food. Watson rolls forward and you both get in. Klaus has his hands full with an enormous burger so it's lucky that Watson can drive himself. Your boss takes a bite and you tell him what you've seen. "Hmm," he says. "So, should we go and talk to Nigel Rigmarole next?"

? Do you agree with Klaus that you should talk to a magical expert?

Turn to page 68

KING NIGEL

? Or do you suggest going to Folly Heights in search of Enid?

Turn to page 26

A FAMILIAR MONKEY

BARKING UP THE RIGHT TREE

SITTING IN THE PASSENGER SEAT, you can feel your skin crawling. You're sure that Watson has fleas, but you've never found the courage to mention it, not least because you also strongly suspect that Klaus has them too. You switch on the radio to distract yourself from the itching.

"This is your Lunchtime DJ, Howling Wolf Howard. And talking of lunchtime. Aa-ooo!" The DJ plays the sound effect of a chicken squawking and then being suddenly silenced. At least, you hope it's just a sound effect. You never know with Shady Side Radio. "And the story on everyone's lips this lunchtime is … what has happened to the missing magic?"

Watson lets out a little whine.

"It's OK, boy, we'll find it." Klaus puts his foot down on the accelerator and whispers to you, "I think he's always hoped that some kind wizard will find the right spell to turn him into a dog again. Mind you, much as I liked him as a dog, he's more useful as a car."

The DJ continues. "Here to discuss the news is roving reporter, Gretchen Barfly-Sewer ..."

"Hello," says the scratchy-voiced banshee.

"So, Gretchen. Any idea how this awful accident could have happened?" asks Howling Wolf.

"Accident? This is no accident, despite what that old fraud Franklefink would have you believe. Any experienced magic-wielder will tell you that it's theft – pure and simple."

"I see. If this is about ultimate power then surely it can't be a coincidence that the Enchantress Enid is in town to rally her League of Evil," says the DJ.

"Yes, and just imagine what she could do with all that power," says Gretchen.

"I assume you'll be following this story throughout the day in the *News of the Unusual*?" asks the DJ.

"I would but the printing press runs on magic, doesn't it?" replies Gretchen tetchily. "We can't print a thing. But if I could get the paper out, I would be reminding my readers that this happened on Dimbleby's watch. As Head of the Magic Circle he should take full responsibility."

"Thanks, Gretchen," says the DJ. "And we'll be right back after these messages."

Funny jingly music starts playing and you hear another voice say, "I'm Nigel Rigmarole and what I don't know about magic isn't worth knowing. Come along and visit Nigel's Elftronics Emporium for all your magical household appliances and repairs. One wave of my wand and you'll wave goodbye to your daily chores!"

Klaus switches it off.

Driving across town in a car that used to be a dog is unnerving at the best of times, but with no magic, the roads are even more chaotic than usual. You had no idea how much the Shady Side relied on magic but even the traffic lights are out. A burly UPF troll is trying, and failing, to direct traffic. He is blowing his whistle angrily at a school bus, which is refusing to give way to a coachload of goblins.

Klaus pulls Watson to the kerb and leaves him sniffing a lamp post. Snark Park is a patch of overgrown wasteland with a small dark wood and a murky expanse of water known as Lake Stench at its centre. You would rather avoid this place but Klaus explains why you're here.

"The headquarters of the Magic Circle is located directly below the city," he says. "Usually, magic folk just zap in and out, but there are a couple of pedestrian entrances and one of them is in the middle of this park."

You are grateful for the presence of your enormous yeti boss as you follow the winding path into a dense fog. There's something unnatural about the way it hangs in the air. A few steps further in and you can't see a thing … but you can hear them. Howls and hisses. Rattles and growls. You walk as closely to Klaus as you can but it's especially hard to see him as his white fur blends with the mist. He suddenly stops and you walk right into him, which is rather like walking into a large, hairy pillow that smells of body odour and fast food. You're about to ask him why he's stopped when you hear a lisping voice.

"Mister Thnuggles. Mister Thnuggles!"

You see a red shape in the mist. As you draw closer, you see that it is a spotty dress worn by a little girl.

"Oh, hello? I've lost Mr Thnuggles." She peers up at Klaus. Sensing that she is not a Shady Side resident, Klaus pulls his collar together, giving the impression that he is a large man in a fur coat rather than a yeti. This must be enough to fool the little girl because she doesn't stare or scream. She simply looks at you and asks, "Have you seen Mr Thnuggles? He'th about thith big." She holds her hands up to demonstrate and you notice that she is clutching a dog lead. "I do hope he'th all right. He's thuch a wee little thing – only a baby really."

"That's good. They tend to spit out the little ones," Klaus quips.

"What do you mean?"

"Nothing," Klaus says. "You really shouldn't be walking your pet on your own around here."

"I know but my naughty friend left a window open and now Mr Thnuggles hath run away. Poor thing."

"We'll keep an eye out for Mr Snuggles," Klaus says.

"Thank you," says the little girl. She looks at you and you see a spark of mischief in her eyes. Where are her parents? What is she doing in the middle of this misty park all on her own, upset but not scared? Before you can ask about any of this, she vanishes into the mist.

You continue on your way, wondering how on earth Klaus knows where he's going. You can barely see your own hand in front of your face. Eventually he reaches a clearing. At the centre is a single tree with silvery-white bark.

"This is the one," says Klaus. "If I remember correctly, this tree is a lever that opens up an entrance around that rock over there."

"You remember correctly but I'm afraid you can't do that," says a voice behind you.

You spin around.

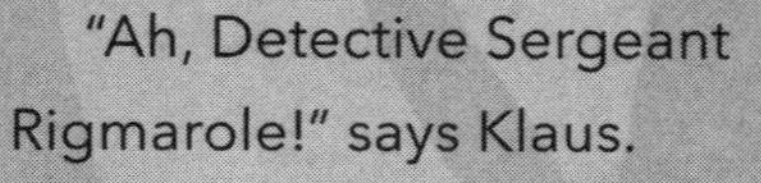

"Ah, Detective Sergeant Rigmarole!" says Klaus.

"Actually, it's Detective Inspector Rigmarole now," she replies.

You have met this elf before. She answers to a minotaur by the name of Chief Inspector Darka. She stands almost as tall as Klaus because she walks on stilts, hidden under her neatly ironed blue trousers.

"Wow. Another promotion, Elphina," says Klaus. "Congratulations!"

"Thank you, Klaus. But I can't let you use this entrance. No one goes in. No one goes out. Those are my orders."

Klaus sniggers. "So Darka is hoping to solve this one, is he?"

"Chief Inspector Darka is currently on holiday. My orders came straight from Night Mayor Franklefink," replies Rigmarole. "He doesn't want this situation affecting Magicon, but have you seen the chaos this is causing already? The town is full of witches and wizards and half of them can't do a thing without casting a spell."

"What about you?" says Klaus. "Aren't all elves magic-wielders?"

"We all have the ability but we don't all practise. I'd rather be judged on my own merits."

"Very admirable," says Klaus. "So how is standing by this tree helping you solve this crime?"

"I'm covering for one of my troll officers," says Rigmarole. "But don't worry, I'm all over this case like warts on a witch's face. We have officers rounding up the prime suspects for questioning."

"Any joy getting hold of Enid yet?" asks Klaus.

"No, but she's on the list. She's been causing trouble like this for years. Remember that time she turned the moon into a bowl of milk?"

"Yes, all the werewolves started meowing," chuckles Klaus. "And then there was that time she made it rain frogs."

"Everyone was hopping mad about that one," says Elphina. "We're keeping her apartment at Folly Heights under surveillance, but it's not going to be easy to find someone who can change her appearance at the drop of a hat," says Rigmarole. "For all I know, you're Enid."

"For all I know, she's you," says Klaus.

Rigmarole smiles. "Or maybe she's listening to us both."

They both turn to look at you. It's unnerving. You take a step back and stumble on a root. Rigmarole chuckles, and Klaus smiles as he helps you up.

"I'm sorry," he says. "Are you OK?"

You nod. Your pride took a knock but you're fine apart from that.

"I was actually thinking your dad might be worth talking to," says Klaus. "He knows everything about magical energy."

"Please leave my parents out of this," says Elphina.

"Oh yes, how is your mother? Sandra's still working for the Council, isn't she?" Klaus sounds like he is casually chatting to a former colleague, but you understand that there's always a reason for his questions.

"She's District Governor now," Elphina replies. "She was busy enough with Magicon before this magical mishap. Also, she's been a bit stressed about Dad recently."

Klaus's nostrils flare. "What about Nigel?" he asks.

Before Elphina can reply, you feel a sudden violent jolt. The earth shakes, sending you staggering to the side.

"What was that?" asks Klaus.

"Erm ... goblin mining crew. It's nothing to worry about."

"Really?" says Klaus doubtfully.

"Forget the goblins, Solstaag." Elphina sounds keen to change the subject. "Look, I can't let you down into the Magic Circle headquarters – I have orders. But if you really want to help solve this thing, go after Enid."

"Thanks for the advice," says Klaus. "Good luck with your investigation, too. I'd say let the best detective win, but I think we both know who that would be."

"I seem to recall your assistant cracking the last case you had," replies Elphina, winking at you.

"What can I say? We're a good team. See you around, Riggers."

Klaus turns and walks away. Your boss used to work for the UPF and there is still plenty of competitive spirit between them when it comes to solving crimes. You wonder how honest Elphina was being with you. You've never met anyone who didn't have at least a couple of secrets stashed away. She certainly didn't like it when Klaus suggested you might interview her father.

Klaus whistles. Watson beeps his horn in response and drives across the patchy grass to join you. The ground is soft and his wheels skid, sending mud splattering behind him. He comes to a squelchy stop and you climb inside.

"I think she's right. We should head to Folly Heights to see if we can find Enid," he says. "What do you think?"

? Do you agree that you should try to locate Enid?

Turn to page 26

A FAMILIAR MONKEY

? Or would you rather speak to Nigel Rigmarole?

Turn to page 68

KING NIGEL

MOONDANCE THE RADIANT

THE HAVENTRY EXHIBITION CENTRE USUALLY plays host to boring events such as home insurance conferences and meetings of the International Pencil Appreciation Society or the annual Dishcloth Collectors Convention, but occasionally it gets booked by the Shady Side community. Magicon requires a huge venue with lots of rooms for the events, panel discussions and demonstrations scheduled over the weekend.

There's a steady stream of cars entering the car park. Magic or not, everyone is getting ready for the big event. Watson finds a parking space a short walk from the main entrance.

"This is the calm before the storm," says Klaus. "Even though the official opening ceremony is tonight there are still lots of smaller events happening today."

On the other side of a pair of sliding doors, a security man in a yellow jacket sits behind a desk. He looks up at Klaus from his newspaper.

"Hello. Gosh, you're a big fella. How can I help you?"

"I'm looking for the unicorn healing rooms," replies Klaus.

The man smiles. "You lot make me laugh," he says. "Second corridor, third room on the left. Oh, and nice costume, by the way." The security guard turns to you. "What is he?"

"I'm a yeti," says Klaus. "Thanks for your help."

"A yeti," says the man, as you're walking away. "So, like the abominable snowman?"

"He's a second cousin, actually," replies Klaus.

The security man laughs. He thinks Klaus is joking. He has no idea he just had a conversation with a real-life yeti. You sometimes wonder what it would take for people like him to believe in the kinds of things you now take for granted.

"Ah, here we are," says Klaus as you find the door.

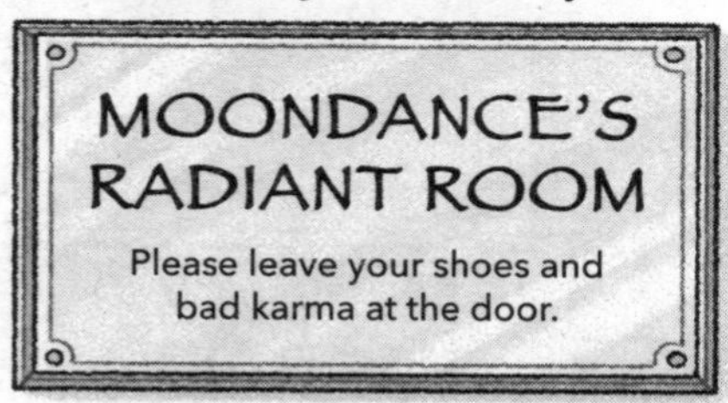

MOONDANCE'S
RADIANT ROOM
Please leave your shoes and
bad karma at the door.

Klaus turns the handle and enters. The first thing that hits you is the smell. Candy rose petals and freshly baked bread. A fine mist hangs in the air. Soothing harp music plays. As you follow Klaus, you find your arms sway in time with the lilting melody. The whole place is designed to make you feel relaxed.

"Hey." Klaus clicks his fingers in front of your eyes. "Are you with me?"

You blink and wiggle your head, trying to shake off the desire to curl up on one of the beanbags that are dotted around the room.

"Welcome to the heart of relaxation," sings a soothing voice.

A silvery horn appears through the mist. You hold your breath as you catch your first glimpse of the unicorn's face. He bows his mighty head and you see his milky eyes. When you exhale it comes out as a sigh.

"Ah, new friends. Thank you for reaching out to me." The unicorn maintains eye contact. "I'm afraid you've just missed this morning's relaxation session. The next one starts in an hour."

"We're not here to relax," says Klaus.

"You're fans, are you? Oh, very well."

As usual, you have your notebook at the ready. To your surprise, Moondance lowers his horn and does a wiggle on the paper. When he steps back you see he's written his name in multicoloured bubble writing.

"We're not autograph hunters," says Klaus. "We have a few questions to ask about the missing magic."

"Magic is never missing when you're with a unicorn." To prove it, he moves his head in a circular motion, drawing a rainbow in mid-air with the tip of his horn. You gaze at it in wonder.

Moondance prods the rainbow with the tip of his horn. It shatters with a shimmering *POOF*, like a miniature firework.

"Magic," gasps Klaus. "How is that possible?"

"Unicorns are not magic-wielders like witches and wizards. We are magical creatures. Like phoenixes and dragons, we make magic while we sleep."

"So Haventry's magic being stolen hasn't affected your powers?" says Klaus.

"That's right, but I fear it will disrupt this weekend's programme," he says. "Magic is vital to our process. These healing rooms are a safe space where members of our community can learn to wipe the slate clean and become the best versions of themselves. Tell me, are you the best version of yourself?"

The unicorn is addressing you. Thankfully, before you can give the subject too much thought, Klaus says, "The fact that you have magic puts you on our suspect list."

"Suspect list?"

"For stealing the magic."

"Why would I do that? I don't want to take magic. I want to share it. Magic is a gift and yet so many of our kind feel we must hide our powers from the rest of the world. We unicorns want to share the magic. As far as we're concerned magic is love. It's for everyone."

"Can you prove this isn't the stolen magic you're using?" asks Klaus.

"Unicorns don't deal in proof," replies Moondance. "We are mythical creatures of wonder."

"Yes, but you're not above the law." Klaus walks around the unicorn, glancing about the room. You're trying to take everything in too but the smell of burning incense is making your head feel heavy.

"Magical creatures do not even follow the laws of nature. Why would we obey laws made by mere humans?" says Moondance.

"Such as those made by Night Mayor Franklefink, you mean?"

"What a dreary man he is," sighs Moondance. "He's introducing all these new laws because he wants to control what he doesn't understand, and that's pretty much everything. I heard it was Sandra Rigmarole, the District Governor, who organized the whole of Magicon, but Franklefink is making it all about him. He's apparently got some announcement planned for the opening ceremony although goodness knows what that is. Something about his precious monsters, no doubt."

"Maybe we should talk to Sandra Rigmarole about the missing magic, see if it's connected to Magicon in some way," says Klaus.

"If you really want to find the thief I'd head down

to the Magic Circle headquarters to look for clues," says Moondance. "That's what I'm going to do now. I can take you if you wish."

"How?"

"Simply place a hand on my flank and I will transport us all there."

"Give us a moment, would you?" says Klaus.

Moondance nods respectfully and takes a step back. Klaus crouches down to whisper in your ear.

"We do need to get into the Magic Circle headquarters to find out more, and right now this hippy horn-head is our best way there."

You understand Klaus's point but you hesitate. You're looking at the name *Sandra Rigmarole* in your notebook. She does sound as though she knows what's going on behind the scenes, and you could really do with talking to someone like that right now.

? Do you want to go to the Magic Circle?

Turn to page 85

THE MAGIC CIRCLE

? Or would you rather visit Sandra Rigmarole?

Turn to page 76

THE 99TH FLOOR

WHILE MOST OF HAVENTRY'S HUMAN residents buy their toasters, kettles and TVs from the electronics superstore in a retail park on the outskirts of town, Shady Side residents buy their gadgets from Nigel's Elftronics Emporium. All the same things are available, but rather than being powered by electricity they run on magic.

"Nigel Rigmarole has had this store for as long as I can remember," says Klaus. "He's a bit of a local character. Everyone knows him. He has these silly adverts where he shows off his latest gadgets. As you know, his daughter Elphina works for the UPF, while his wife Sandra has been climbing up through the Shady Side Council for years."

You try to jot this down but he's talking fast and Watson is hurtling around a roundabout. You feel a little carsick and you're glad when Watson comes to a skidding stop outside the shop.

It doesn't look like much from the outside. Even on the inside it isn't instantly obvious what's remarkable about a small store crammed full of electrical equipment on floor-to-ceiling shelves.

Closer inspection reveals that these aren't your average electrical items. You spot a werewolf grooming kit, a vampire fang brush and a zombie brain whisk. Nigel stands behind the counter on a stool, one hand resting on his round belly. You suspect there are several chins hidden under his thick beard. He wears a blue overall and has a long purple feather behind one pointy ear and a phone receiver held to the other. Behind him, you notice hundreds of plain white boxes stacked up.

"Yes, I understand that the washing machine has stopped working but, as I have already told you, all my items are guaranteed, except for when there is no magic ... No, it's all there in the small print."

You can't hear what the voice on the other end is saying but, from the pitch, you can tell that this is not a happy customer.

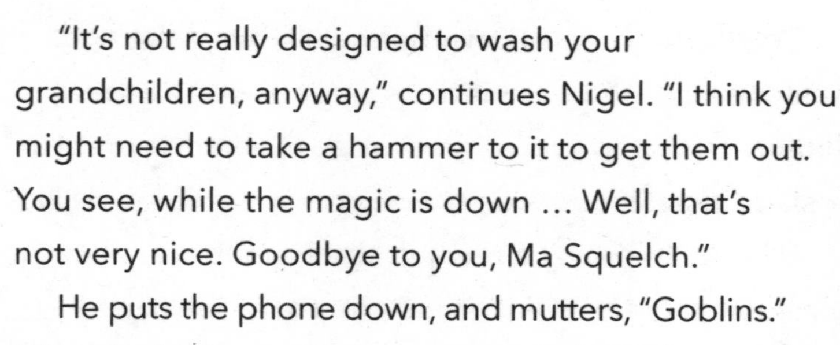

"It's not really designed to wash your grandchildren, anyway," continues Nigel. "I think you might need to take a hammer to it to get them out. You see, while the magic is down … Well, that's not very nice. Goodbye to you, Ma Squelch."

He puts the phone down, and mutters, "Goblins." When he looks up, he notices you and your boss. "Ah, Klaus Solstaag, how are you? Has Watson's battery gone flat again? If so, he'll have to wait. Usually I'd do a quick charging spell, no bother." He pulls the feather from behind his ear and waggles it around. "But, I don't know if you've heard, there's a problem with the—"

The phone rings, interrupting him. Nigel snatches up the receiver and snaps, "Nigel's Elftronics Emporium, what can I—" You hear someone shouting angrily through the receiver.

"Well, yes. You can try turning it off and on again but it still won't work because, in case you haven't heard, THERE IS NO MAGIC!"

He slams the phone down.

"Honestly," he says. "My customers!"

"We're trying find out what happened to the magic," says Klaus.

The phone rings again.

Nigel picks it up, shouts, "Yes, I know there's no magic!" then slams it down again. "These people want their everyday problems solved by magic, but they have no clue how it actually works."

"Has this ever happened before?" says Klaus.

Nigel gives a slightly awkward cough. "Not for a long time. Anyway, did you know that we do magical repairs now?" He holds up a business card. Klaus takes it and hands it to you. "You have to diversify to survive, you see. Magic rates keep going up so I'm having to do everything I can to keep the business afloat. I just hope the magic is returned soon, so business can go back to normal, but they'll have to get it off the thief to do that."

"Can't someone, er, you know, make some more magic?" asks Klaus.

"Make more magic?" exclaims Nigel. "Magic can't just be magicked out of nowhere. To generate the amount needed to run this city would usually take months."

"So where does magic come from in the first place?" asks Klaus.

"It's all very technical." Nigel picks up a screwdriver and fiddles with the back of a clock. "Let's just say it comes from under the ground. But don't worry. My Elphina is running the UPF investigation." Nigel pounds his chest proudly. "She takes after her mother, that one."

"How is Sandra?" asks Klaus.

"Busy. Franklefink swans around making speeches and coming up with new laws, but it's Sandra who has to do all the actual work. If it wasn't for her, I don't think Magicon could have happened at all, but does she get any credit from that man? Not a drop. It's typical of how humans treat elves, but I'm going to change all that."

"Change it how?"

Nigel's grin widens. "You are talking to the direct descendant of Elron, the last king of the elves."

Klaus bursts out laughing.

"You can mock all you like, but this is real and the coronation is happening this evening. It's about time us little people had a true leader – instead of a Night Mayor with dodgy deals and unfair taxes – and I'm the elf for the job."

"How do Elphina and Sandra feel about it?"

Nigel squirms a little. "They've been very supportive."

Klaus is still chuckling but your mind is racing with possibilities. You never know what will turn out to be relevant. Could Nigel's claim to be king be connected with the missing magic?

You wonder if Klaus is thinking along similar lines when he says, "You never struck me as someone interested in seizing power, Nigel."

"I only want what is rightfully mine, and to build a better world. At least I'm not rallying my followers to rise up and destroy it."

The phone rings again. Nigel answers.

"Listen, I know the— Oh, sorry, love. It's turning out to be one of those d— Oh, really? Late again? Yes, but don't forget the coronation … That's not fair. This is important to me. You have your career. Elphina has hers. I have this. This is my legacy. It's *our* lega— Sorry, yes, I know you're busy. I'll see you this evening, my sweet."

He hangs up.

"Sorry," he says. "What was I saying?"

"I think you were suggesting that Evil Enid might be behind this theft," says Klaus.

Nigel scratches his chin thoughtfully. "She certainly seems like the most obvious candidate to me. Elphina thought so too, but I don't know if she—"

Nigel breaks off to answer the ringing phone.

"Nigel's Elftronics Emporium, how can I help you? Ah, it's you. Listen, I've been thinking about this deal and I'm not sure that it's really ..." He places a hand over the receiver. "Sorry, this is going to take some time. It's a business associate. Good luck with the case, Klaus. The sooner we find the thief, the better." He goes back to his phone call. "Sorry, yes. Now, about my percentage."

You follow Klaus out of the shop, your mind buzzing. You're not even sure which of the names on your list are suspects. Perhaps none of them. It could be anyone. There are so many possibilities.

Outside the shop, Klaus turns to you.

"So once again things are pointing to Enid. Maybe we should head over to Folly Heights." Klaus lifts his hat off and uses it to fan himself. "Is it me or it is getting warmer?"

It does feel like the temperature is rising, but maybe it's just that you're feeling the pressure of this case. The more you travel around town, the more you see signs of how things are falling apart without magic to hold them together. Across the road from Nigel's shop a pair of wizards are mid-argument, each accusing the other of having stolen the magic. They've both drawn their wands but, with no magic, they're forced to use them like swords. They look like a couple of kids fighting with sticks. You look down at the two names you've circled in your pad. But who should you go after next?

? Do you want to look for Evil Enid?

Turn to page 26

A FAMILIAR MONKEY

? Or do you want to seek out Sandra Rigmarole?

Turn to page 76

THE 99TH FLOOR

THE ENTRANCE TO THE SHADY Side Council building is next door to the City Chamber, where members of the Shady Side community gather to discuss local matters. Klaus pushes a pair of double doors open and you step into the reception where a gnome sits behind a desk, a pencil in his mouth and the *News of the Unusual* crossword in front of him.

"Hi, there," says Klaus.

"Six across," says the receptionist. "Ten letters. Explosive contains capable snowman."

"Explosive means bomb," says Klaus. "Another word for capable is able. So *a bomb in able*. The answer is abominable."

The gnome looks up at him, impressed. "Oh yes. Very good. Thank you."

"Where would I find Sandra Rigmarole?" asks Klaus.

"Ninety-nine down," says the gnome.

"Is that the next word you need?" asks Klaus.

"No, that's where her office is. She's on the ninety-ninth floor, but the District Governor won't usually see people who just walk in off the street."

"I'm an old friend," says Klaus. "She'll see me."

"OK, then," says the gnome brightly. "You can take the lift."

"Thanks," replies Klaus.

You walk across the atrium and press the button to call the lift.

"Two down, three-seven, a colourful but misleading fish," calls the gnome.

You try to beat Klaus to the answer.

"Red herring," he says over his shoulder.

The gnome scribbles in the answer. He's pleased to be making progress with his crossword, but you have a much more complex puzzle forming in your own notepad. In both cases, an early mistake can throw everything off that follows. The real trick is to watch out for the places where the different clues link up. You know those crucial connections are where you'll find the solution to this unfolding mystery.

As the organizer of Magicon, wife of Nigel, and second in command after Franklefink, Sandra Rigmarole connects in all kinds of ways, so you're hoping this interview will shed some light on the case.

"The council offices are all below ground," says Klaus. "The more important the official, the lower the floor. Sandra is only one floor away from Franklefink himself. She's worked hard to get herself there too. I've known Sandra a long time so leave the talking to me."

You always do. Your boss's strength is his ability to tease out truths from those who would rather keep them hidden. Yours is your ability to watch, listen and piece together the strands of truth until you weave them into something that leads you to the solution.

The further the lift descends, the hotter it gets. When the elevator stops, you can feel sweat on your forehead. You can tell that Klaus is bothered by the rising temperature.

"There must be a problem with the air conditioning," he says. "Maybe that needs magic to work too."

You're panting as you step out and walk down a corridor with various offices along it. You stop outside a door with gold letters that read:

Klaus knocks on the door.

"Yes?" says a voice.

You step inside to see an elf in a smart business suit behind a desk that is full yet rigorously organized. Unlike Klaus's desk, the piles of paper are carefully sorted into sections labelled *Inbox* and *Outbox*, with colourful stickers marking pages, and you notice she has different pots for different-coloured pens. As you enter, she's signing a document with a long quill.

"Ah, Klaus Solstaag." She places the quill behind her ear. "Uh-oh. Please don't say that Franklefink is so desperate that he hired you to recover the magic. I remember what happened the last time he hired you to sort out his problems."

"Me too," says Klaus, a little edge to his voice. "We sorted them out."

Sandra Rigmarole looks at you. She smiles and you spot the family resemblance between her and her daughter. They both have keen green eyes, full of spark and ambition.

"Franklefink didn't hire me," says Klaus, "but I am trying to find out what happened to the magic."

"There's no need. I have absolute faith in my daughter's ability to crack this case. Elphina is a detective inspector now. That's the same rank you reached before you were fired, isn't it, Klaus?"

"I retired. I wasn't fired," says Klaus. "I wasn't suited to life in a uniform. I'm not very good at blindly following orders."

The conversation is interrupted by a low rumbling. The ground shakes.

"That keeps happening," says Klaus.

"Oh, it's nothing, just a goblin mining crew. They're working on the air conditioning."

"That would explain the heat." Klaus mops his brow, sprinkling you with droplets of sweat.

When you hear a *PING!* you assume it comes from the computer, but Sandra Rigmarole opens a drawer and pulls out a small, stripey pole. As she tips it up, it makes a whooshing noise like a rain stick, then it says in a small, wooden voice, "As popular as a dog whistle at a werewolf disco."

"What is that?" asks Klaus.

"It's an opinion pole. It lets me know how we're doing with the community," says Sandra, with a terse smile. "As you can tell, we're not faring well. The loss of the magic is causing all kinds of problems."

"What a remarkable object." Klaus reaches out to examine the pole. "How does it work?"

"Very well, thank you." Sandra pulls it away and places it down on the desk. "Now, do you have a point?"

"We're here to help. We want to find out who took the magic as much as you." Klaus softens his tone. "Come on, Sandra, you can trust me with anything – I've known you and your husband a long time."

"I know, Klaus. I'm sorry. I am rather busy." She sighs. "I suppose you've heard this nonsense about Nigel claiming to be king of the elves? Ridiculous elf."

Klaus nods but doesn't reply. You often marvel at how well he can extract information from people just by allowing them to talk without interruption.

"Even if he can trace his history back to Elron the Great, so what? The same is probably true of half the elves in Haventry. And we've moved on from kings and queens. These days, we choose our leaders. Although not always the right ones in my opinion." She shakes the pole again.

PING! "As popular as a kraken in a mermaid salon," says the pole's voice.

"Oh dear. That's a record low," she says. "Franklefink won't like this."

Yet again, the room shakes. This time the quake lasts longer and sheets of paper fall from the desk. You bend down to pick them up, glancing at the sheet on top.

OPERATION OVERTHROW
THREAT LEVEL ANALYSIS
TOP SECRET

"That is confidential council business," says Sandra, snatching it out of your hand. "Now I really do have a lot of work to do. And this problem with the, er … goblins. I should get on top of that."

"Thanks for your help."

As soon as the door closes behind you, Klaus says to you, "She's not telling us everything, but then I imagine working so high up – or rather low down – for the council, she must have her share of secrets."

You tap Klaus on the elbow. It's not that you aren't listening. It's just that you've noticed a sign.

MAGIC CIRCLE® HQ
THIS WAY
⟶

"Well done. This is too good an opportunity to miss," says Klaus. "We may have other people and places on our list, but right now, we need to get to the scene of the crime. Just hold on to your faculties because the journey into the Magic Circle headquarters can be a bit ... er, confusing."

Klaus opens the door and you step into swirling mist. You lose your footing, trip and tumble inside.

Turn to page 85
THE MAGIC CIRCLE

THE MAGIC CIRCLE

STEPPING INTO THE HEADQUARTERS OF the Magic Circle feels like being dragged upside down through an hourglass, while being spun around on your head. You want to scream but when you open your mouth, no sound comes out. As you slowly rematerialize, you look down at your hands to reassure yourself that they are still attached to your arms. To your relief, you are in one piece.

You look up and see the long face of a white unicorn with a pink mane.

"I, Moondance, welcome you to the inner sanctum of the Magic Circle," he says. He draws a wave of rainbow colours in front of you with the tip of his horn. With a whoosh, the wave becomes a circle that gradually fades and vanishes. "Did you know that all rainbows are circles if seen from the right vantage point?" He sighs. "It's all a matter of perspective."

"Perspective is a useful thing in the detective line of work too," says Klaus.

"Ah, Klaus Solstaag," says an old man with a long beard and pointy hat. "I wondered how long it would take for you to turn up."

As your eyes adjust to the dim lighting you can see you're standing in a windowless room with dark brick walls and a heavy wooden door with metal hinges. You recognize the wizard standing next to the unicorn as Grand Master Dimbleby. He's holding a candle and his hand is shaking so much that the flames flickers wildly.

"Sorry," he says. "Usually this place is lit magically but we're forced to use these infernal contraptions!" While talking, the wizard accidentally puts his finger in the flame. "Ow!" He shoves the finger in his mouth to cool it down. Unfortunately, as he does this his sleeve catches fire.

"Good to see you, Dimbleby," says Klaus, clapping his hands over the sleeve to put the fire out.

"You too," says the wizard. "And Moondance, to what do we owe the honour?"

"I thought you might need some assistance with this situation," says the unicorn. "Since I still have my magical abilities maybe I can shine a light on things." He bows his head and his horn touches Dimbleby's hand.

"Ow!" Tiny sparks fly and the wizard releases the candle. Instead of dropping to the floor, it drifts up into the air and glows twice as brightly.

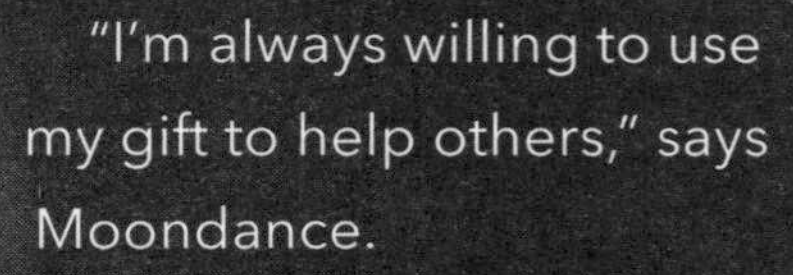

"I'm always willing to use my gift to help others," says Moondance.

"Thank you," says Dimbleby, examining his finger. "Unicorns generate their own magic, you see," he says, turning to you and Klaus. "It's all held in their ... what's-a-ma-called ... in their ... the things on their heads."

"Our *horns*," says Moondance. "Oh dear, is the stress of this awful situation getting to you, Grand Master? I did hear some disturbing rumours that some in our community are even calling for your resignation. The world of magic can be so cruel at times."

"I've been doing this job for over seventy years and I don't think I've had a day when someone didn't call for my registration ... No, what's the word? Resignation," says Dimbleby.

"Seventy years? You must be exhausted. Allow me to make you a refreshing rainbow smoothie," says Moondance, magicking a brightly coloured glass from nowhere.

Dimbleby waves it away, so Moondance whooshes it into your hand.

"Help yourself," he says. "Rainbow smoothies are exquisite but they never last very long."

You put your mouth to the straw and drink. You feel as though your tastebuds are exploding.

Weirdly, it's exactly how you've always thought a rainbow would taste – delicious.

"Grand Master Dimbleby," says Klaus. "We're here to help but we need you to be honest with us."

"During my time in charge of the Magic Circle, we have always been as transparent as possible. And I'm not just talking about invisibility spells." He strokes his beard as he chuckles.

"Then you won't mind taking us to see the scene of the crime," says Klaus.

"Of course," says Dimbleby. "Anything to get the magic back."

As he leads you down the shadowy corridors, you take in every detail. The walls are decorated with ancient hieroglyphics and mysterious symbols. There are cubbyholes filled with intriguing artefacts and ancient objects. If these walls could talk, they would tell stories of powerful potions, scheming sorcerers and wicked witchcraft.

You hear a rumbling and feel vibrations through the soles of your feet. Dust falls from the ceiling. It's another earthquake. You stagger back and feel

Klaus's hand on your back, preventing you from falling.

"What *is* going on?" asks Klaus.

'It's just the goblin mining crew," says Dimbleby.

"So much for transparency," whispers Moondance.

"What does that mean?" asks Klaus.

"Nothing," says Dimbleby firmly, glaring at the unicorn. "The problem we need to focus on right now is the missing magpie … er, magic."

"If you're having problems with your memory, I can show you a meditation to help," says Moondance.

"There is nothing wrong with my members' club … I mean, my memory. Ah, here we are." Dimbleby looks relieved to have arrived at a large, ornate door. He tries to open it, but it won't budge, so Klaus steps forward to push it.

"Thank you. Usually, I'd use magic," admits Dimbleby, "but as you can see, the abraca-router has been completely drained."

In the centre of the vast, round room, a huge metal circle hangs from a heavy chain. A pair of fairies are pacing around it, waving their wands at it, occasionally causing little sparks to fly.

"Is this really where the magic comes from?" asks Klaus.

"Comes from?" A fairy laughs. "No, the abraca-router harvests the magic, stores it and distributes it."

"So where *does* it come from?" asks Klaus.

"Er …" The two fairies look at one another, unsure how to answer.

"It's all very technical," says Dimbleby quickly. "It involves ley lines and things."

"That's something of a simplification, isn't it, Cabbage?" says one of the fairies.

"It is indeed, Moss," says the other. "This ring usually holds around sixty thousand kilo-whizzes of magic, drawn from the—"

Dimbleby coughs.

"From the natural mystical force of *ley lines*," says Cabbage, although you wonder what he was going to say.

"What is a ley line?" asks Klaus.

"I like to think of them as power lines for the earth's magic," says Cabbage.

Moss wrinkles his nose at that description and adds, "But since it's Magicon this weekend, we tweaked the abraca-router to hold around one hundred thousand giga-whizzes!"

"Which is a lot of magic," says Cabbage.

"Enough to turn the sun into a sandwich," says Moss.

"So where is that magic now?" asks Klaus.

"Inside the magical conductor of whoever stole it," says Moss.

"Magical conductor?" says Klaus.

"Usually a wand," says Cabbage, waving his around. "But it could be anything really." He indicates Grand Master Dimbleby's huge wooden staff.

"It could be a unicorn horn," says Moss.

Moondance gives a dismissive whinny.

"And is this room guarded?" asks Klaus.

"The door has always been triple-locked and bolted," says Dimbleby.

"Which is pretty pointless since most magical folk could transport themselves inside the room anyway," says Cabbage.

"There's supposed to be someone watching it," says Dimbleby, "but it's been such a long time since anything like this happened, I think everyone got too relaxed about it."

"I did mention this possibility in my last report," says Moss.

"Yes, well, it's easy to say with hind legs ... sorry, hindsight," says Dimbleby. "But I honestly thought Enid had moved on from this sort of caper."

"So you think it was her too?" says Klaus.

"I don't see who else would want to do such a thing," says Dimbleby.

"Yes, and Enid has always been trouble," says Cabbage.

"I suppose she has," admits Dimbleby, "but even though she's the Empress of Evil, I've always found her very amenable."

"What about you two?" Klaus addresses the pixies. "Do you think Enid is behind this?"

Moss and Cabbage consider the question.

"It could be anyone," says Moss, thoughtfully scratching his chin. "Well, anyone with a good knowledge of magic and a thirst for unimaginable power."

"Assuming it was taken on purpose," says Moondance. "It could have been an accident."

"Actually, that's really not very likely," replies Moss.

"It's still possible, though," replies Moondance.

"Whoever stole it, we need the conductor they used," says Cabbage. "Once we have that, we can put the magic back and get the abraca-router up and running."

He leans forward and speaks in your ear, so the others can't hear, not even Klaus. "As soon as you have the conductor, you need to hold it aloft and say:

**"Cauldrons bubble, fires burn,
Now the magic must return."**

You scribble down the words but you're halfway through the last one when another earthquake strikes. The magic ring swings like a giant pendulum. You dive to avoid it, but the ground splits and you to scramble to get back as a crack snakes its way across the floor.

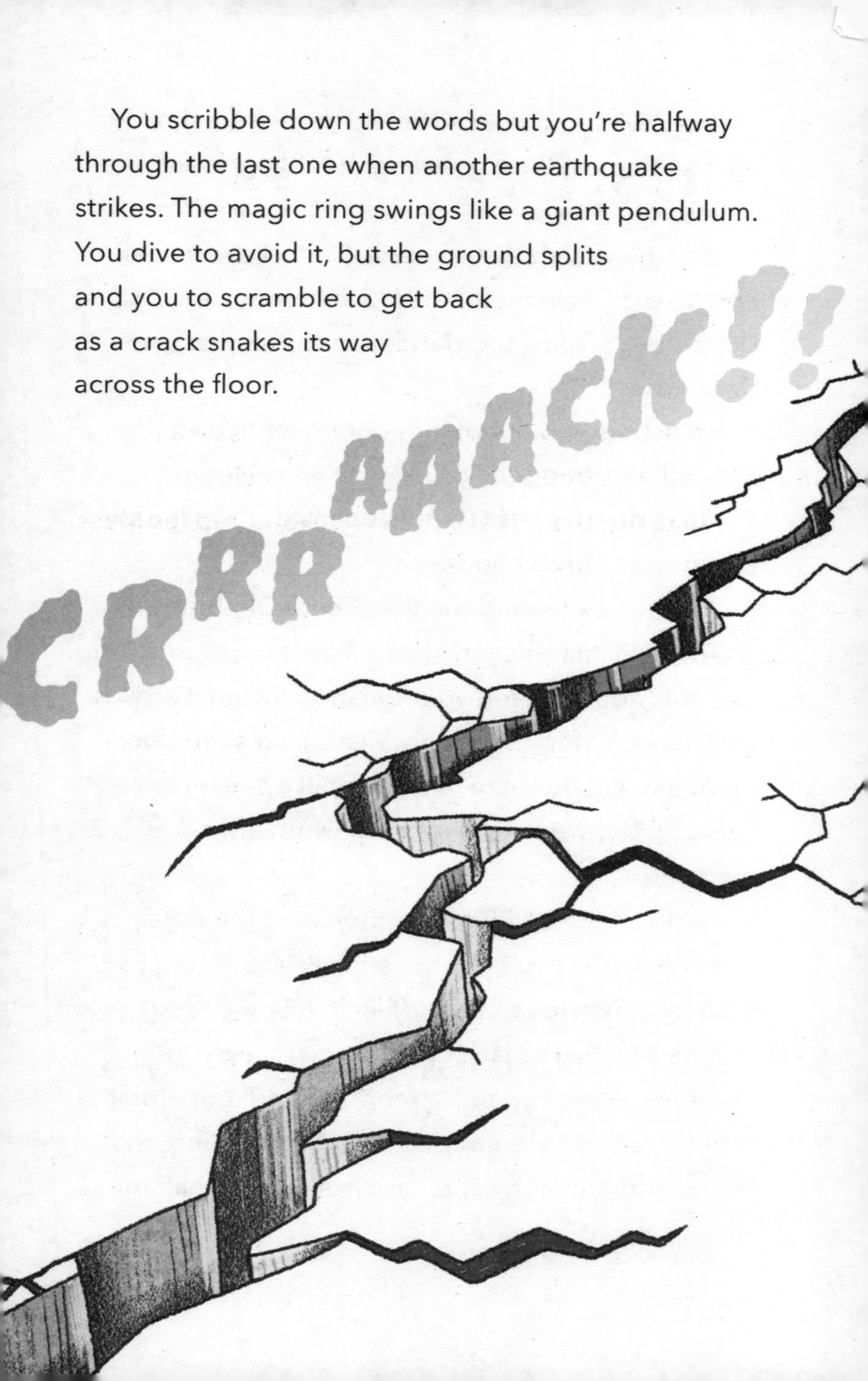

You cover your eyes to shield them from the dust and hear a loud growling, rumbling sound that rattles your bones.

"I'm sorry. With these quakes, I must ask that all non-Magic Circle members leave immediately," says Dimbleby. "It's just too dandelion ... No, that's not it. Dangerous!"

He ushers you out of the room over to a lift. He slides the door open.

Klaus doesn't hesitate to step inside. "I'm happy to get out of here," he says.

"Good luck finding the thief," says Dimbleby.

The door slams shut. The lift hurtles upwards. You grip the sides to keep your balance. When it arrives at the top, it stops suddenly. Klaus slides the door open and you breathe in fresh air. It's a relief to see sunlight, but you're still shaking when a shadow falls over you.

"Hello, Klaus." UPF officer Elphina Rigmarole peers down at you from her stilts. "Ha. So I see you found a way into the Magic Circle HQ, then."

"We did," says Klaus.

You're expecting to be reprimanded, but Elphina smiles. "Good," she says. "Franklefink is piling on the pressure to solve this case but I've got half my officers dealing with the problems caused by these quakes and the other half trying to cope with this missing magic business. I'm at my wit's end. What a week for the chief to go on holiday. I need your help, Klaus."

"We're more than happy to work together on this, aren't we?" says Klaus, looking at you.

You nod and hand your notebook to Elphina. She looks at all your case notes so far.

"Er, why are my parents' names down here?" she asks.

"We're trying to keep our options open at this stage," replies Klaus. "Your mum is high up in the council these days and your dad knows a thing or two about magic."

"Listen, Mum wants this solved as much as we do, and all Dad cares about is his stupid coronation. King of the elves, last descendant of Elron the Great ..." She sighs. "I love him dearly, but he's as daft as a brush. As I told Franklefink, there's no way he was involved in any of this."

Klaus grunts quietly but doesn't interrupt.

"I appreciate you're being thorough, but everything is pointing to Enid as far as I'm concerned," says Elphina.

"So everyone keeps telling us," says Klaus. "But where's the evidence? All I've seen so far are assumptions."

"Oh, come on, she's been missing for hours. She must know everyone suspects her, so why hasn't she come forward? Innocent people don't run and they don't hide."

"I agree. It is suspicious. We haven't come across her either," says Klaus. "At least, I don't think we have. I suppose you can never tell with someone who can change their appearance at the drop of a hat."

Elphina looks around then lowers her voice. "Listen, Klaus. I've received word that Enid is holding a secret meeting scheduled to start in half an hour in the room above Brockley Jacks. I was going to go myself – it's our best, maybe only, chance of finding her – but now Franklefink's insisting I attend a press conference and I need to prepare. It's almost like that man cares more about looking like he's solving the crime than actually solving it."

"We'll check out the secret meeting," says Klaus.

"Thank you. If you really want answers you'll forget about my parents and go find Enid," urges Elphina.

Your conversation is interrupted by a voice from the woods.

"Mr Thnuggles! Oh, Mr Thnuggles!"

You glance over your shoulder and spot a little girl wearing a red spotty dress and clutching a dog lead.

"That girl and her dog," says Rigmarole. "She's been looking for it for hours now and you know what kinds of things lurk in these woods. If she's not careful it will be more than her dog that goes missing."

She hands your notepad back. You follow Klaus towards the road. He's moving with purposeful strides, but you keep glancing at the little girl calling for her lost dog. You notice that she has a basket hooked around her arm. It's quite far away but it looks to you as though the blanket inside it is a little singed around the edges. Maybe it's your imagination but something bugs you about it. All good detectives trust their gut, and yours is churning away like a cement mixer. But what is it telling you? What should you do?

? Do you want to go to the secret meeting?
Turn to page 113
THE SECRET MEETING

? Or do you want to follow the little girl?
Turn to page 106
A GOOD CAR CHASE

YOU BARGE THROUGH THE DOOR so fast you almost fall down the steps. You steady yourself on the banister and keep moving. It's hard to believe a little girl could move so fast. The walls of the stairwell are lined with posters showing acts who have played in the theatre above Brockley Jacks: dragon baiters, a magician called the Great Impossible, a zombie clown's one-man live show – *Undead 'n' Funny*. By the time you reach the bottom, it's too dark to see anything.

You reach out your hands and find a door. Pushing it open, you step into a large hall lined with stone pillars. The whole place looks as though it could do with a lick of paint. Flickering candlelight reveals cracked walls. Even the bunting strung from the ceiling looks like it's seen better days.

When you see a pair of shadowy figures at the end of the hall, you dive behind a pillar. One is a large-bellied elf, the other a wild-haired human who wears a white lab coat and a large gold chain around his neck.

"Listen, Franklefink. You might get to order my wife and daughter around but this is one Rigmarole who's free to do what he wants."

"Nigel, Nigel, Nigel," says Franklefink. "No one is ordering anyone around. I'm just asking you to postpone to avoid the clash. We can't have the elves here when they should be at the opening ceremony. You of all people should understand how important it is. As the council's main repair elf, you stand to make a lot of money from this."

"Yes, about that. As I told you on the phone, I'm not happy with the amount you're offering me."

"If you can't handle the business then I'll find someone who can," says Franklefink. "After my big announcement tonight I fully expect this new venture to go global. Today, Haventry. Tomorrow, the world. And you will be a part of it. How exciting is that?"

"Always bigging yourself up, aren't you?" says Nigel.

"You're one to talk about bigging himself up," says Franklefink. "Really, Nigel? What is this nonsense about being an elf king anyway?"

Rigmarole puffs out his chest. "I am doing this because it's time we elves stood up for ourselves."

"You mean just as Elron stood up for himself?"

"Yes ... well, not exactly like that."

"You may well squirm," says Franklefink. "My people have done their research. I know what Elron did, which does make one wonder whether you could be involved in this whole magic-theft business."

"How dare you." Nigel pulls out a long purple feather and waves it in Franklefink's face. "You should be grateful there isn't any magic around right now."

"Are you threatening me?" says Night Mayor Franklefink, nervously backing away from the feather.

The two men circle each other, maintaining eye contact. You're listening intently, trying to piece everything together. You wonder what Elron, the last of the elf kings, could have done that would make Franklefink glower so suspiciously at Nigel.

"Don't go accusing me," says Nigel. "For all I know you're trying to cover your own tracks. Remember, I know how much magic you need for the opening ceremony. I wouldn't even put it past you to have done one of your dodgy deals and got someone to steal the magic on your behalf."

"That's ridiculous," says Franklefink. "My deals are never dodgy. And remember, you're soon to benefit from one of them! This new venture will put

Haventry on the map. So please drop this bogus claim to royalty."

"Bogus! Listen, Franklefink!" Nigel is now shouting so loudly that his face has turned purple. "I am having my coronation tonight whether you like it or not. I am the heir of Elron and I fully expect the entire elf community to gather and celebrate the dignified crowning of their new king. So there." He blows a raspberry.

Night Mayor Franklefink pulls out a hanky and wipes his face, then leaves through a door by the stage.

It's time for you to go too.

Your heart is beating fast as you run back up the stairs. You consider what you just witnessed. What deal have these men struck? What is this new venture Franklefink mentioned? Could either of them be responsible for the missing magic? Your mind is awash with ideas, questions and suspicions. You must get back to Klaus to share your thoughts and come up with a plan of what to do next.

"I AGREE THERE IS SOMETHING odd about a little girl walking around on her own, especially on this side of town," says Klaus. "Maybe it's nothing but let's go and have a chat."

However, as soon as you follow the girl, she speeds up. She's surprisingly fast. It's hard to tell if she knows she is being followed but you suspect that she does.

"Excuse me," yells Klaus. "We'd like a word."

He breaks into a run. You do the same but struggle to keep up. Your boss's huge feet make the ground shake as he runs. The girl reaches the road and jumps into a taxi that's waiting by the kerbside. Klaus whistles for Watson and his faithful car jumps into action, reversing the wrong way down a one-way street then performing a perfect handbrake turn and skidding to a halt.

"Come on," he says. "We haven't lost her yet."

You pause to pick up something on the ground. It's the dog lead that the little girl was holding. There's a collar at one end – it has a metal tag with the words Mr Snuggles printed on it. You pick it up and turn it over to find the initials *E.E.E.* scratched into the back. You drop it into your bag.

"Hurry up," snaps Klaus.

The passenger door pops open and you jump in. The wheels spin and you're off. Watson loves a good car chase. You've always thought you would enjoy the experience too but, as with so many aspects of detective work, the reality is distinctly more terrifying than how it looks in the movies.

You drag the seat belt over your shoulder and click it into place as Watson takes a sharp right turn. Klaus tries to slow him down by slamming his foot on the brake but Watson is in hot pursuit.

"Ideally I'd like to still be in one piece when I catch up with her," says Klaus.

Watson isn't listening. He's swerving in and out of the heavy traffic as though it's a game. A siren sounds. You've attracted the attention of a police car. And it's not the UPF. How can you explain to a human officer of the law that your car used to be a dog and you're currently chasing someone you hope might help you solve the mystery of the missing magic?

Thankfully, Watson's erratic driving means you

lose the police car as easily as you picked it up. But the Shady Side is busier than ever. You've never seen so many long, flowing robes or pointy hats. With no magic, witches and wizards are being forced to walk and no one looks very happy about it. A bunch of witches have strapped their broomsticks to the backs of bicycles, but they obviously have no idea how to ride them and keep swerving all over the place.

The taxi comes to a screeching halt outside a pub called Brockley Jacks and the little girl darts inside.

"This is where the evil secret meeting is taking place," says Klaus. "Now what would a sweet little girl be doing visiting a meeting of the most dangerous wizards and witches in the world?"

You jump out of the car and run after her. As you pass through the pub, Klaus waves at the bartender. You take the stairs two at a time, but everyone else is heading in the opposite direction. An angry crowd of witches and wizards is piling out of the room and down the steps.

"The whole thing is a shambles," says an elderly wizard. "All we want is Armageddon. Is that too much to ask?"

"Yeah, well, ah'm-a-geddin' out of here," replies a witch. "Who wants to sit around and listen to that monkey? Not me."

"I'm thinking of giving up being evil altogether," says another.

"Oh, don't say that," she replies. "You love being evil."

"I know. I just wish Enid would show up and tell us what's going on."

You push through the crowd and finally reach the room, but the girl is not there.

A monkey in a top hat stands on the stage. "Please don't leave, everybody," he cries. "Even without Enid here, there is still much valuable work we can do. I've put together a presentation about Operation Overthrow."

Klaus stops, turns and says, "An innocent little girl is hardly going to accidentally end up at a meeting where this bunch of evildoers are plotting to take over the world. Something's going on and we need to find out what. She must have taken one of those doors."

He points to a pair of doors labelled *NO EXIT* and *NO ENTRANCE*.

"We'll take one each," says Klaus. "But we'd better be quick."

? Do you want to go through the door marked No Exit?

Turn to page 101

NO EXIT

? Or the one that reads No Entrance?

Turn to page 122

NO ENTRANCE

You've visited Brockley Jacks before. The ground floor is a grotty one-room pub with dusty curtains and a sticky carpet, but the room above hosts some of the Shady Side's more extraordinary live performances. From the slapstick of zombie clowns to the deadpan humour of ghost comedians, all the weirdest entertainment occurs upstairs, but this afternoon it's been hired out for a secret meeting of the League of Evil.

When you arrive, a witch is standing by the door holding a clipboard. "Hello, my dears. Are you here for the secret meeting?"

"Naturally," says Klaus.

"I just have to check before you go in that you

are both registered users of evil magic, intent on wreaking havoc and upsetting the natural order of the world."

"Er …" Klaus glances at you and shrugs. "Yes?"

The witch ticks a box on her form. "In you go, then."

Entering the room you see posters, all with the same picture of Enid, with her long black hair falling over her shoulders. She looks terrifying, and so do her followers. The room is awash with long, greasy hair, oily skin, warty faces and crooked teeth. They cackle and crow. They rub their hands together and wave their wands. You are relieved there's no magic available. These are the wickedest of the wicked. And they are not happy.

Standing on a wooden chair on a small stage is a monkey wearing a waistcoat and top hat. He waves a black walking stick in the air as he tries to get the room's attention.

"Evil witches and wizards," he says. "As many of you know, I am Mr Charles Evans, the appointed familiar, apprentice and loyal servant of the great and all-powerful Enid the Evil Enchantress. Can I get a HEY HO!"

However, his efforts to gee up the crowd are not well received.

"We know who you are, chum," yells a red-faced wizard, banging his staff on the ground. "We're here to see the organ grinder, not the monkey."

"Organ grinder? Oh, I see, as in the expression. Yes, very funny," says Mr Evans. "Although, technically I'm not a talking monkey. I'm a man who has been transformed into a monkey in order to ..."

The boos and jeers of the crowd drown him out.

"Where is she?"

"Did she steal the magic?"

"Is it all part of her plan?"

The crowd is getting riled. Mr Evans raises his hands but he's clearly struggling to get the ugly mob under control.

"Listen. No one's more upset about this than me. I truly believe in our evil cause. But if you calm down I do have some very exciting news to share of what's coming up— Ow!"

A tomato lands right between the monkey's eyes. More fruit follows. A rotten apple flies past your ear. The crowd surges forward and you lose sight of Mr Evans until you spot him crawling out between their legs. He pokes his head up from under a wizard's purple robe, looks at you and says, "Help!"

"Follow me," says Klaus.

He quickly leads the monkey to a door with a star on it. You slip inside and Klaus closes the door behind him. Inside the room is a mirror surrounded by light bulbs.

"We'll be safe in this dressing room for the moment," says Klaus. "That's a pretty angry bunch out there."

"They're livid," says Mr Evans. "But what can I do? I haven't seen Enid all day."

"You must have some clue what she's up to."

"None at all, I'm afraid."

Fists pound on the door. "We know you're in

there, you useless primate. Tell us where she is!"

"They want to tear me to pieces," sobs Mr Evans. "Limb from limb! But I'm just the scape-monkey. It's Enid they want."

"No one is tearing anyone to pieces on my watch," says Klaus.

The banging and yelling get louder. Klaus still has his hand on the doorknob, holding it closed, but you can tell he's struggling.

"I'm going to open the door now," he says loudly. "But there will be no lynching."

"Not even a little bit?" replies a wizard.

"Not even half a lynch. Understood?" says Klaus, sounding rather like a schoolteacher.

"Oh, all right, then," says the wizard.

Klaus opens the door. A couple of witches stagger in, pushed by the force of those behind them. The crowd goes quiet as they stare at the monkey, then the purple-faced wizard says, "We want our money back."

"Yeah," says a red-haired witch. "Hold on, what money? This was a free event, wasn't it?"

"True," admits the wizard, "but I did have to catch the bus to get here."

"Listen," growls Klaus, "we want to find Enid as

much as you. If she's behind the magic theft, we need to track her down, so if anyone knows anything about her whereabouts, I highly recommend you come forward now."

"We haven't seen her since coffee this morning," replies a green-skinned witch.

"I was expecting her to be here," says another.

"I want to hear about Operation Overthrow," adds a third.

The monkey says, "Listen, I'm looking forward to overthrowing the establishment and replacing it with a reign of fear as much as the rest of you, but we must be patient. Knowing Enid as I do, I daresay she has some sinister scheme up her— Ow!"

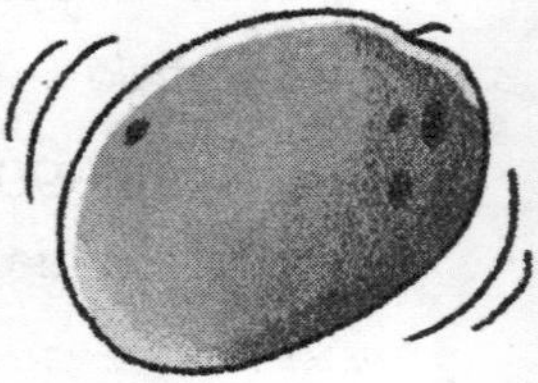

An overripe mango hits Mr Evans right between the eyes.

"I saw who threw that," he says. "And I'm taking your name off the guest list for the Sinister Shindig tonight."

"Shindig?" says Klaus.

"Our drinks party before the opening ceremony. And I'm sure Enid wouldn't miss that," he says, although he doesn't look sure at all.

"I'm not staying here to listen to this waffle," says a wizard.

"Yeah, let's go," says another.

"No, please stay," says Mr Evans. "Even without Enid here, there is still valuable work we can do. I've put together a presentation about Operation Overthrow."

But no one wants to listen to the monkey. As the room gradually empties, you spy a red spotty dress at the back. It's the same young girl who was looking for her dog. What would she be doing here among these evil magical folk? You slip through the crowd, but she notices you and turns to get away.

You lose sight of her briefly as a pair of witches try to get past. Barging your way between them, eager to catch up, you stumble and trip. There's something on the floor – a dog lead. Picking it up, you read the tag: *Mr Snuggles*. You turn it over in your hand and read the initials *E.E.E.*

"It looks like we finally have a lead with this case." You look up to see a wry smile on Klaus's face. "But where did she go?"

There are two doors. One says, *NO EXIT*. The other says, *NO ENTRANCE*.

"You take one. I'll take the other," says Klaus.

Which do you choose?

? Do you want to go through the door marked No Exit?

Turn to page 101

NO EXIT

? Or the one that reads No Entrance?

Turn to page 122

NO ENTRANCE

BEHIND THE DOOR, A STONE staircase leads upwards. You bound up the steps as fast as your feet will carry you. At the top is a flat roof with a metal barrier around the edge, but there is no sign of the little girl.

You dash over and peer down. There she is, standing in the street below. You bang your fist on the barrier in frustration, turn and head back down the stairs, through the pub and out into the road. There are still a few witches and wizards milling around, but the girl has gone.

However, you've spotted something else of interest.

Grand Master Dimbleby enters a doctor's

surgery across the road from the pub. Whether it's a werewolf with a sore throat, an unravelling mummy, or a yeti with a head cold, if any of the Shady Side community has a health problem, they all go to see their local GP, Dr Iris.

So why is the Head of the Magic Circle taking time out in the middle of a crisis to see the doctor? Klaus isn't there to discuss what it might mean so you follow your instincts. There's too much at stake to rule out anything that might shed light on this situation. You cross the road and arrive at the surgery at the same time as a goblin called Ma Squelch and her chaotic assortment of grandchildren.

"Come on, you lot," she says. "In you go."

You follow them inside and slide down on to a chair in the waiting room as the goblins sneeze all over a zombie traffic warden and a particularly pale-looking vampire. Grand Master Dimbleby sits opposite you, reading *Which Wand?* magazine.

"May I help you?" The receptionist is a ghost dressed in a flamboyant feathered hat and frilly shirt.

For a moment you panic that she's talking to you. You're relieved to realize she's scowling at Ma Squelch.

"Yeah, my grand-gobbles have got a case of the sneezle-splats."

"Have you made an appointment?"

"No, I have not," says Ma Squelch. "But if you don't treat them, your whole waiting room will be dripping with goblin snot."

She has a point. The goblins haven't stopped sneezing since they entered. One of them has sneezed his way on to the ceiling fan. You grab a magazine to shield yourself from the snot shower and from the harsh glare of the receptionist.

"You'll have to wait your turn," she says. "Grand Master Dimbleby, the doctor will see you now."

"Ah, thank you." The ancient wizard places his magazine back on the table and leans heavily on his staff as he gets to his feet. You bury your nerves, then follow. Klaus has taught you that if you ever want to go somewhere you're not supposed to be, it pays to act naturally. The more you try not to be seen, the more you get noticed. You try to ignore how fast your heart is beating as you fall into step behind Grand Master Dimbleby. Anyone watching would assume you were with him, but the wizard hasn't even noticed you behind the sway of his robe.

As soon as you step inside the surgery, you dive under a table.

"Hello, Dr Iris," says Dimbleby. "Thank you for seeing me."

The doctor is a cyclops. She looks up from her computer and blinks – or maybe it's a wink. It's hard to tell. "No problem at all. Now what can I do for you today?"

"Yes, well. It's a rather delicate matter," replies Dimbleby.

"It's just you and me," says Dr Iris. "You can talk freely."

"I keep getting my words jumble-saled ... I mean, jumbled up," he says.

"I see," says the doctor. "And when did you first notice this?"

"I can't quite remember," admits Dimbleby. "I would suspect it's the result of a confuddle spell but I can't see how it can be as there's no margarine ... Er, magic."

"Hm, may I ask how old you are?"

"Two hundred and twelve."

Dr Iris lets out a whistle. "Well, that is impressively old, even for a wizard," she says. "Have you thought about the effect stress might be having on you these days? Could you perhaps step back from your duties?"

"Retire?" says Grand Master Dimbleby. "I wish I could, but who would replace me?"

"I'm sure I don't know," says Dr Iris, "but your health should come first. Now, let's do a quick test. Take a look at these two pencils." She holds up one blue and one red pencil. She then places the red one behind her back.

"What colour pencil did I just remove?" she asks.

"Colour?" says Grand Master Dimbleby. "I'm afraid I wasn't looking at the colour."

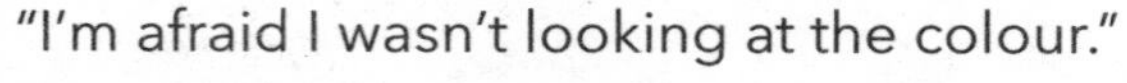

"Hm." The doctor shows Dimbleby the pencils again. He peers at them, then she puts the blue one behind her back. "Which colour did I remove this time?"

"Oh, darn it. I forgot to look at the colour again. Green, maybe?"

Dr Iris tuts. "I think I'd better refer you to a specialist. I'd definitely say this is something you need to keep an eye on. Try to take it easy – this problem could well go beyond muddling your words."

The room shakes. Another earthquake is striking. A framed certificate on the table above you falls and smashes on the ground.

"What *is* that?" asks Dr Iris. "It's been happening all d—"

She is interrupted by an explosion of goblins entering the room.

"I'm so sorry, doctor." The receptionist floats in after them. "I couldn't stop them."

All three goblins sneeze at the same time, sending a pile of snot straight into Dr Iris's eye. It must be disgusting for her but it affords you the opportunity to run out of the surgery. As you hurry down the road, you hear the honk of a car horn. Watson pulls over and you jump in.

As he drives you back to the office, you pull out your notepad and stare down at your confused scribblings. What have you just learned? You already knew that Dimbleby was muddling his words, but now you can tell he's more concerned by his memory than he's been letting on. Has Dimbleby forgotten a vital clue? Could it be that he somehow drew the magic from the abraca-router by accident? How likely is it that Dimbleby was the cause of this disaster and doesn't even know it himself? Or is there another explanation? Whatever the truth, you need to get back to Klaus.

THE BETTY PROBLEM

THE OFFICE IS UNBEARABLY HOT. Klaus looks like he's just stepped out of a shower. The smell indicates otherwise.

"I can't understand this heat," he says. "It was lovely and chilly this morning." He uses an old newspaper to soak up the sweat then lobs it at the bin. "I need something to eat."

He reaches into one pocket and pulls out half a sandwich. He quickly seasons it with a sachet of pepper from his other pocket then shoves it into his mouth. Your boss often has food on him and it does seem to help enliven him as you tell him what you've just seen, but you can tell he's not really taking it all in.

"I'm sorry," he says. "It's so hot I can't think. I hope you have some ideas."

It makes you nervous that Klaus is relying so much on you. He has more confidence in you than you have in yourself. You sit down at your desk and take out your notes, looking at the list of the suspects you wrote down at the beginning and all the people you've met since. Everyone's a suspect until proven otherwise. That's what Klaus always says. Everyone has something to hide. You're staring at your notes when you feel a rumbling.

"Watch it," says Klaus. "Another tremor is hitting."

You're trying to steady the lamp on the desk when the door swings open. Bootsy, the witches' monster, lumbers in, making the office shake with every step. "Sor-ry," he moans.

"Move, you big useless lump," says Burnella Milkbird, barging him out of the way.

"Have you always had this many stairs?" asks her sister Bridget.

"Yes, but this is the first time you've actually walked up them," says Klaus. "What do you want?"

"We're here to help you solve the case before it's too late," says Burnella.

"What do you mean *too late*?" Klaus mops his brow.

"So you haven't found out about Betty, then?" says Bridget. "Some detective you are."

"Who's Betty?" says Klaus.

"She's one of Haventry's best-kept secrets," says Burnella. "We're only letting you know now because you need to understand how urgent it is that we find the thief."

"Know what?" asks Klaus.

"Haven't you been wondering about these quakes?"

"Yes, but … Just tell us," he growls.

"All right, all right, keep your fur on. Betty is the dragon who slumbers beneath our city," says Bridget.

"There's a *dragon* under Haventry? Since when?" Klaus glances at you, eyes wide. This is news to you both.

"Since forever," says Burnella. "Like unicorns and phoenixes, dragons generate magic while they sleep, and Betty has been the source of the abraca-router's power for two thousand years."

"Dimbleby said it had something to do with ley lines," says Klaus.

"Why do you think they're called that?" says Bridget. "They're lines made by where dragons lay down."

"Isn't it a bit dangerous placing a city on top of a dragon?" asks Klaus.

"It's perfectly normal. Pretty much all major cities are built on some kind of giant magical creature. Keeping them asleep means we have a steady supply of magic and it stops them from roaming about attacking humans."

"Why doesn't she wake up?" asks Klaus.

"That's where us Milkbirds come in," says Burnella proudly. "For generations, our family has made a magical potion that keeps the dragon asleep. This would have been a crispy fried city years ago if it wasn't for us. But she needs a regular supply and, with no magic available, we can't make any new potion."

"Which means Betty is waking," says Bridget. "She's rising up and getting closer to the surface – didn't you wonder why it's getting so warm?"

Another quake hits, knocking a picture off the wall.

"The unicorn still has magic," says Klaus. "Can't Moondance put her to sleep?"

"Oh no. Unicorn magic is far too refreshing for sleeping potions," says Burnella.

"Maybe he should try talking to her." Bridget snorts. "That would send me off."

"We have another question about the theft," says Klaus, ignoring Bridget's joke. "Dimbleby mentioned that someone stole the magic once before, but we don't know who or when."

"Oh, that was Elron," says Burnella.

"The last elf king?" Klaus looks at you. "The one Nigel claims is his ancestor?" He picks up a fan and tries to move the propellors round with his finger to create a breeze. When this fails to work, he drops it back on to the desk. "Elron stole the magic?"

"Yes, but that was centuries ago," says Burnella. "These days everyone just sees elves as makers and fixers, no one takes them very seriously, but they were the first creatures to learn how to wield magic – long before humans got involved. Elron wanted to take it back – all of it. His plan was to steal the magic for the elves, then use it as a weapon in a war against humans."

"And if Nigel is his descendent, maybe he has the same idea," says Klaus.

"Nigel is a big joke … well, a little joke, I suppose,"

says Bridget. "It's his wife who's the real problem. Sandra Rigmarole has ideas above her station. Unelected busybody. She wanted to shut down our League of Evil coffee mornings, but we have rights."

"Rights? You're plotting the destruction of the world," exclaims Klaus.

"It's called freedom of speech," says Bridget. "Not that Sandra Rigmarole understands that. It's lucky Franklefink overruled her."

"Interesting," says Klaus. "So Franklefink and Enid get on, do they?"

"Franklefink understands that being evil is a lifestyle choice. It doesn't mean you're bad," says Bridget.

"Baaaaad," moans Bootsy.

Burnella turns to you and says, "So how are you going to find the thief?"

An idea hits you. Remembering the free guide to Magicon in the *News of the Unusual*, you grab this morning's newspaper and flick through to find the guide.

"Good thinking," says Klaus, taking it and opening it to today's date. You glance at the clock. There are three events scheduled to start in fifteen minutes.

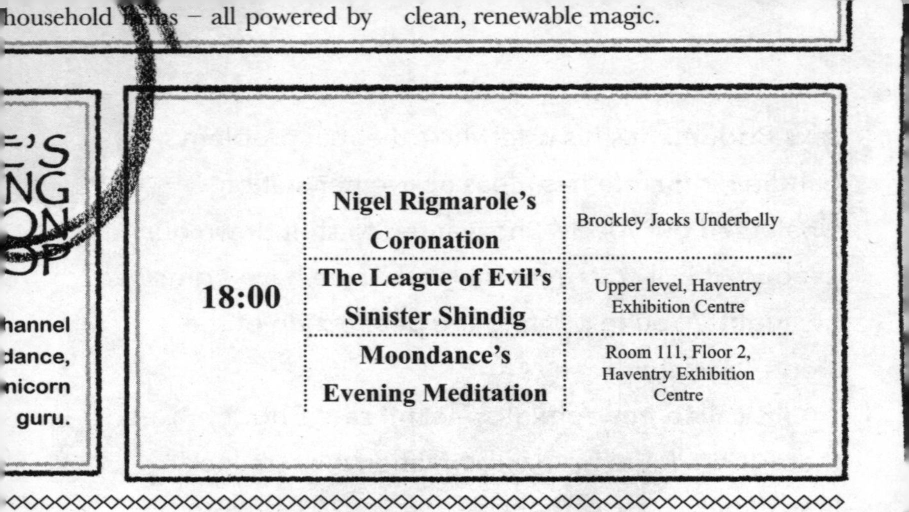

household [illegible]s – all powered by clean, renewable magic.

18:00	Nigel Rigmarole's Coronation	Brockley Jacks Underbelly
	The League of Evil's Sinister Shindig	Upper level, Haventry Exhibition Centre
	Moondance's Evening Meditation	Room 111, Floor 2, Haventry Exhibition Centre

"If I were you I'd be going to Franklefink's press conference," says Bridget. "This whole thing stinks of an inside job to me. Franklefink might not have a magical bone in his body but he's always cooking up some scheme or other and I've heard that he needs a lot of magic for whatever he's got planned for the opening ceremony."

"Making monsteeeeer," moans Bootsy.

"Yes, yes, yes," says Burnella. "I think Bootsy rather fancies his chances with Franklefink's latest creation but I keep telling him, Franklefink is making Enormelda for himself."

"He only ever does anything for himself, that man," says Bridget. "Anyway, I'm not hanging around here any longer. Some of us have plans."

"Evil plans?" says her sister.

"So what if they are?" replies Bridget before storming out of the room. Bootsy goes after her, like a monstrous pet following his owner.

Burnella lingers long enough to whisper urgently in your ear. "I don't trust her. She's more loyal to the League of Evil than she is to her own flesh and blood. I don't know where she's going now but if you think Enid is behind this crime, maybe you should be following my sister."

Burnella clicks her fingers, clearly expecting to disappear dramatically, before remembering that there's no magic. Embarrassed, she huffs and hurries out of the room.

"The way I see it we have four options," says Klaus. "Nigel Rigmarole, evil Enid, Moondance the unicorn or Franklefink's press conference. What do you want to do?"

? Do you want to go to Nigel Rigmarole's coronation?

Turn to page 158

THE CORONATION OF KING NIGEL

? Or would you like to see if Enid turns up at the Sinister Shindig?

Turn to page 178

PARTY CRASHING

? Or would you like to go to see the unicorn?

Turn to page 152

MOONDANCE'S EVENING MEDITATION

? Or attend Franklefink's press conference?

Turn to page 145

PRESS CONFERENCE

? Or should you heed Burnella's warning about her sister? There's still time…

Turn to page 139

NUMBER 13 BUS

"**YOU WANT TO FOLLOW BRIDGET** Milkbird? Are you sure?" Klaus is staring at you like you've lost the plot. You're beginning to wonder if you have. "She wasn't on my suspect list," he continues. "Listen, I trust you, but I don't think we can put all our eggs in one basket so I'll check out the press conference and meet you at the Haventry Exhibition Centre afterwards."

You nod and run down the stairs and into the street. Steam rises from the cracks in the pavement. There's a continuous rumbling sound. You're suddenly filled with doubt. Now is not the time to go it alone, and yet that's precisely what you have done.

You spot Bridget hopping on to a bus. Burnella

and Bootsy are standing by their caravan. Wherever Bridget is going, she's on her own.

The bus bell chimes as it pulls away. You don't think twice. You run after it.

"Hey, watch it, bud!" yells a pixie on a unicycle, suddenly swerving to avoid you.

There's no time to say sorry as you run after the bus. On the back of it is the number 13. This black bus with darkened windows is exclusively used by the Shady Side community. If anyone from the other side of town dared board it, there's a good chance they would never be seen again.

But you are different. This job has changed you. You're braver than you ever imagined you could be. You've learned to take your chances and follow your instincts. With a sudden burst of energy, you jump and grab the cold steel pole at the back of the moving bus. You swing inside and go flying through a ghost. The sensation of passing through a spirit is usually unnerving, but you're so hot that the fleeting chill to your bones is a welcome relief. You mop the sweat from your brow, apologize, then head up to the top deck.

You spot Bridget sitting next to a short man in a top hat. The seat behind them is empty. You make your way down the aisle. A family of vampires turns to look at you as you pass. From the way they hiss, you know they've smelled your human blood. A zombie turns his head all the way around and stares at you, showing you his yellow teeth and blackened gums. You find your seat as quickly as possible and realize that it isn't a man Bridget is sitting next to. It's a monkey in a top hat.

"Mr Evans," says Bridget. "You have to tell me what the plan is. I'm one of Enid's biggest fans."

"They all say that," replies the monkey. "But I'm sorry, I don't know where Enid is. I'm her familiar, not her nanny."

"Oh, come on, you can tell me," pleads Bridget. "Did she take the magic? Is it all part of … you know … *Operation Overthrow*?"

"Shh!" Mr Evans anxiously looks around, checking no one is listening. You drop down in your seat to avoid being spotted.

"Don't say that here," whispers the monkey. "Remember, if we win the vote this weekend, we'll be full steam ahead, but we don't want certain people finding out about it beforehand."

"Franklefink wouldn't dare get in our way," says Bridget.

"Oh, I'm not worried about him. Franklefink's on our side since Enid gave a rather generous donation to his election campaign. Once the magic is back and Operation *You Know What* gets the thumbs up …" He taps his nose. "After that, it's only Dimbleby who could cause us serious problems."

"Oh, he's as useless as a broken broomstick," says Bridget.

"Dismiss Dimbleby at your peril," says Mr Evans. "He's a powerful wizard and he's never been a friend to the League of Evil. He'll do whatever he can to stop us."

When you first arrived on the top deck you

could hear muttering and moaning, but it's eerily quiet now. You glance over your shoulder. Is it your imagination or is that family of vampires sitting closer? The zombie has twisted his head even further around to look at you, the skin at his neck now piled like a corkscrew.

"I bet Enid did steal the magic," says Bridget. "It's classic her. That's what I like about her. She never does anything by halves."

"Yes, but you know what they say," says Mr Evans. "Behind every great witch, there's a great familiar."

"I've never heard anyone say that," says Bridget.

Mr Evans looks rather put out by this. "No one works more closely with Enid than I. We're a team. Remember that time she turned day into night and night into day?"

"Oh yes," chuckles Bridget. "The looks on the faces of those poor, confused vampires were priceless."

"I did the incantation for that," Mr Evans boasts. "She once called me the wind beneath her wings."

"Yes, you are rather like a case of bad wind," sniggers Bridget.

"Haventry Exhibition Centre," says a voice through

the crackly speaker. "All those for Magicon, please alight here, unless you want to attend the opening ceremony, which will be taking place at the next stop, Shady Side Stadium."

"This is my stop," says Mr Evans.

"I'm getting off too," says Bridget.

In fact, almost everyone on the top deck is leaving. Only the family of vampires is remaining and there's no way you're staying with them. You get up and follow the stumbling, mumbling, muttering and moaning passengers off the bus. By the time you get outside you've lost sight of both Mr Evans and Bridget.

The place is swarming with Shady Side folk, milling around the centre. You make your way through the crowd into the building. You need to find Klaus but where should you look for him?

? Should you go to Moondance's Evening Meditation?

Turn to page 152

MOONDANCE'S EVENING MEDITATION

? Or Evil Enid's drinks party?

Turn to page 178

PARTY CRASHING

THE PRESS CONFERENCE IS TAKING place on the steps outside the City Chamber. Watson parks as closely as he can, but the large huddle of people is spilling out on to the road. In amongst the throng of misfits and curiosities, you spot the flame-red hair of *News of the Unusual* reporter Gretchen Barfly-Sewer.

At the top of the steps, DI Elphina Rigmarole stands on stilts at one lectern while Night Mayor Franklefink leans on another. A number of suited council workers watch from behind, including Sandra Rigmarole, who is holding a clipboard in one hand and a stripey pole in the other. Cameras are flashing. Questions are being shouted.

"I have a question for Night Mayor Franklefink!" Gretchen's shrill banshee voice cuts through the noise of the crowd. "What have you to say about the rumours that these quakes have less to do with goblin mining and more to do with the enormous dragon waking up beneath our feet?"

"I'm afraid I don't deal in rumours. The magic will soon be restored—"

"Before or after the city has been burned to a cinder by a colossal fire-breathing beast?" interrupts Gretchen.

You follow Klaus into the throng, but you're much shorter than him and it's hard to see what's going on. You slip out of the crowd to watch from the side. Gretchen's mention of Betty is clearly news to most of them.

"We're all done for!" yells a ghost.

"What do you care? You're already dead!" says a werewolf.

"Please! Everyone needs to remain calm," says Franklefink as the panic builds. "Our experts are working around the clock and I promise that it

will be back in time for my *monstrously* special announcement at the opening ceremony."

"I think we've all had quite enough of your broken promises," says Gretchen. "And no one cares about you or your silly monster girlfriend."

"Oh, you'll care when you hear what I have to say." Franklefink's eyes swivel in his head as he gesticulates wildly. "You'll care!"

Your gaze shifts to Sandra Rigmarole who is listening very patiently, with a blank expression on her face. Her daughter Elphina keeps glancing nervously around. She looks as though she'd rather be anywhere else.

"This question is for DI Rigmarole," says Gretchen.

Elphina gulps and her grip on the lectern tightens.

"How are you getting on with finding the thief?" asks Gretchen. "It must be very hard without Chief Darka to hold your hand."

"I'm not at liberty to discuss our ongoing investigation." Elphina Rigmarole manages to maintain a professional air, but you can tell how much the question rattles her. "But rest assured that we at the UPF and the City Council are working very hard to solve this situation as quickly as possible."

"And this one's for Night Mayor Franklefink," says Gretchen. "Are you worried about how this crisis will affect your popularity?"

You hear a *PING!* and a small voice comes from the pole in Sandra's hand and says, "As popular as a farting troll in a unicorn petting zoo."

Gretchen cackles and you feel her terrible laughter tear right through you.

"No more questions," says Franklefink. "Try to remain calm and—"

The ground rumbles and his words are lost as rubble falls from a nearby building and screams rise up from the crowd. The quakes are worsening. It feels like only a matter of time before a whole building comes down.

"And that concludes the press conference," says

Franklefink. "Don't forget that the opening ceremony will still take place this evening when I will unveil my latest—"

But it is impossible to compete with the growing sounds of panic. The crowd explodes into angry cries of "Tell us the truth!" and "We're all doomed!" Burley UPF troll officers hold the mob back as Franklefink is ushered towards his car, while Sandra and Elphina Rigmarole climb into the back of a taxi which hurtles away.

Klaus is struggling to get through the crowd but you are smaller and able to slip through. You catch up with Franklefink to see a large grey seal wearing a driver's cap holding the car door open for him.

"Thank you, Julian," he says.

"Where to now, sir?" asks the seal.

"Haventry Exhibition Centre," he replies, his eyes narrowing. "I'll show these people that I have their best interests at heart."

"Very good, sir."

The door slams and the car drives away. You run back to find Klaus standing by Watson, holding a door open for you.

"Ah, there you are," he says. "We need to get out of this place."

You agree, but where should you ask Watson to take you next?

? Do you want to follow the Rigmaroles?
Turn to page 158

THE CORONATION OF KING NIGEL

? Or should you be tailing Franklefink?
Turn to page 178

PARTY CRASHING

MOONDANCE'S MEDITATION WORKSHOP IS ON the second floor of Haventry Exhibition Centre. You peer through the window before entering. Moondance stands on a low stage, wearing a headset and microphone to amplify his voice. You spot a couple of pixies, a centaur and a faun but there are plenty of spare beanbags. The lighting is turned down low and gentle harp music plays.

"I'll go in for the workshop."

You turn around. Klaus is bending down so that you're face to face with him. You're glad he's there. You wouldn't want to do this on your own. You work as his assistant, but you often feel more like a partner. He might take the lead in the investigation but so many of the decisions fall to you and it was your choice to come here.

"Slip around the back and look for clues," says Klaus. "I'll cause a distraction so you can sneak in without being seen. Ready?"

You nod and Klaus bursts into the room.

"Evening. Sorry if I'm a bit late. I had terrible traffic and what with these earthquakes ..."

Everyone in the room stares at him. He's ruined the tranquillity.

"Please remove your shoes and find a beanbag," says Moondance calmly.

"I don't wear shoes," says Klaus. "I tried them once but they rubbed my toes and, man, you should have seen the blisters and the scabs."

Moondance maintains his composure as he patiently watches Klaus stumble across the room, slipping on a beanbag and tripping over the kneeling centaur. It gives you the cover you need. You dash into the room and around the back of the stage, ducking down low to avoid being spotted. At least it's cooler in here.

"Right, if everyone is settled," begins Moondance.

"Nothing too strenuous, please," says Klaus. "I'm

already sweating buckets."

"This is a meditation workshop," says the unicorn. "I'll be showing you the basic breathing techniques that will help you find the unicorn within each of you."

Klaus looks down at his belly. "Funny. I don't remember eating a unicorn."

He's doing his best to annoy Moondance so that the unicorn's attention remains on him and he doesn't notice you snooping around backstage. You spot a rainbow-coloured saddlebag. As quietly as possible, you open it up and pull out a scrapbook labelled *PRESS CUTTINGS*. Inside, articles from newspapers and magazines have been cut out and labelled. There are interviews with Moondance, adverts for his meditation sessions and articles that he's written for magazines such as *Which Wand?*, *Warlocks Weekly* and *The Magic Mail*.

"Observe your breath and empty your mind." Moondance continues to drone on and on.

You skim-read the articles, most of which are thinly disguised adverts for his various workshops or self-help books he's written. Then your eyes land on an interview with Gretchen Barfly-Sewer for the *News of the Unusual*.

GRETCHEN: You've been critical of the Magic Circle in the past. Why?

MOONDANCE: I just think it's a shame that they feel the need for such secrecy. Magic should be for everyone, not just the elite.

GRETCHEN: What would you do in Grand Master Dimbleby's position?

MOONDANCE: Probably retire. Ha ha. That's a joke, of course. If I were the Head of the Magic Circle – heaven forbid – I would throw open its doors. No more hiding. I would bring magic to the masses.

You peel off the article and slip it between two pages of your notebook, then drop the scrapbook back into the saddlebag.

"And now we adopt the actualization pose," says Moondance. "Repeat after me, I am focusing on what it is I want to achieve. I can make anything happen. I will bring about change."

Everyone repeats this.

"I am the best unicorn I can be. I will not let down my fans." Moondance chuckles. "That last one is for me. Obviously, if you are unburdened by the pressures of fame, choose your own words."

You poke your head up and catch Klaus's eye as he continues to play along.

"And as we adopt the kneeling position, we say a final thank you to the unicorn energy that flows through us all. And now you may all open your eyes and feel yourselves renewed."

The lights flicker back up, making you jump. Realizing you are out of time, you move swiftly around to the side of the room.

"Well, that was very relaxing, I must say," sighs Klaus, intentionally spoiling the atmosphere so that Moondance is too busy scowling at him to notice you slip through the door. You wait outside, jotting down your thoughts, until Klaus steps out of the room, and reads over your shoulder. He says, "Interesting, though I'm beginning to wonder if the solution to this case has been staring at us since we started. Maybe it was Enid after all. Are you ready to hear my idea of how we might track her down?"

? If you haven't already been to the League of Evil's shindig, maybe you should check for Enid there first?

Turn to page 178

PARTY CRASHING

? Or do you want to hear Klaus's idea of how to track her down?

Turn to page 166

WITCH-SNIFFER WATSON

THE CORONATION OF KING NIGEL

WATSON PARKS OUTSIDE THE SHABBIEST pub on the Shady Side of Haventry: Brockley Jacks. The sign shows a picture of a masked highwayman. It creaks as it swings. You spot Sandra and Elphina Rigmarole slipping through a side door with a sign reading,

ELF CORONATION:
ENTRANCE

"This leads down to Brockley Jacks Underbelly," says Klaus. "It usually gets hired out for birthday parties and wedding receptions. I guess Nigel must be expecting a big turnout for this coronation."

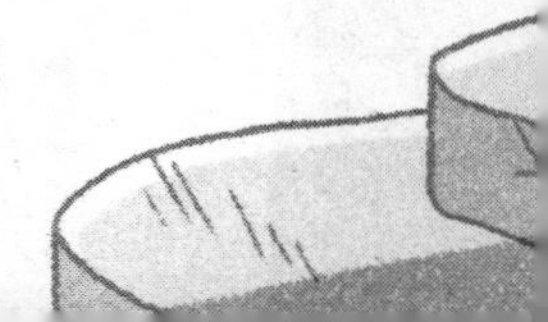

You're expecting to hear the sounds of an excited crowd but, when you reach the door at the bottom, there are only three voices coming from the large hall. Nigel Rigmarole is arguing with his wife and daughter. They're standing on the stage at the end of the empty room. Nigel is dressed in a royal tunic. He carries a golden crown and sceptre on a plush velvet cushion. Detective Inspector Elphina Rigmarole is still in her UPF uniform, but now she holds a tiara in one hand. Her mother Sandra Rigmarole wears a smart trouser suit and a look of exasperation.

"I can't understand it. Where is everyone?" says Nigel.

"Dad, please," says Elphina. "Our community has bigger problems to deal with. There's a ruddy great dragon waking up below us and no magic to help us control the situation."

"She's right," says Sandra. "And most elves are so used to using magic for everything that some of us don't even know how to tie our shoelaces without it."

Nigel looks down at his feet. One of his shoelaces is undone. "Ah, well. It's very tricky."

"Honestly," Sandra sighs and bends down and yanks her husband's laces so tightly that he yelps in pain. "Stay still," she orders.

"What does it matter?" cries Nigel. "No one's here. Not a single elf."

"Maybe you can drop this nonsense now, then," replies Sandra,

"It is not nonsense. I am not silly. This is my birthright," replies Nigel. "It's Elphina's too. And you, my darling, you've always been my queen."

Klaus places a hand on your shoulder. You're standing in the shadow of one of the huge pillars that line the hall. The Rigmaroles haven't noticed either of you. As he often reminds you, you see one side of people when you ask them questions. You see an entirely different side when they don't know they're being observed.

"Dad, you know I love you but Mum is right. Besides, you can't crown yourself king without anyone watching. You'll be a laughing stock."

"Let them laugh," replies Nigel. "Elves need a king. We need something to be proud of."

"You've built a business. You should be proud of that," says Sandra. "And I've worked my way up to District Governor, while Elphina is Detective Inspector."

"You still both take orders from humans."

"Chief Inspector Darka is a minotaur, Dad," says Elphina.

"And Franklefink is a politician," says Sandra.

"And I'm a king," shouts Nigel. "I'm doing this for all elves. With me as their king, we will reclaim the dignity we had before we were just seen as fixers, shoemakers ... and Santa's little helpers! Remember, we are the original wielders of magic."

"You're beginning to sound like Elron," says Sandra.

"At least he put the little people first." Nigel strides across the stage and turns around.

"Elron wanted to take all the magic," says Elphina. "Is it any wonder that you're on Franklefink's suspect list, Dad?"

"Nigel, my love," says Sandra. "If you really care about us, you'll stop this right now. It's embarrassing."

"Oh, I'm very sorry I'm embarrassing you," says Nigel, sounding more offended than sorry. "And now even my own family think I could have done this awful crime."

"We know you didn't do it," says Sandra.

"Absolutely," adds Elphina, sounding less sure. "Enid remains our number-one suspect, but Dad, you need to give up on this coronation."

"Come on, love," says Sandra. "It's time to accept it for what it is." Sandra Rigmarole places an arm around her husband. Elphina stoops to hug them both. It's a tender moment and you feel uncomfortable to witness it.

The same can't be said for Klaus. He steps out of the shadows, revealing your presence to the elves. Elphina is the first to spot him. There's no point in hiding so you follow.

"What do you want, Klaus?" says Elphina.

"The same thing as you. My assistant and I are looking to solve this mystery and, right now, our investigation has led us here."

"Then you're wasting your time," says Sandra.

"My husband is innocent."

"Yes, Klaus, you'd better leave," says Elphina. "I know you're trying to help, but I've told you, you're barking up the wrong tree with Dad."

"Maybe." Klaus glances at you. "I don't know the whole truth but I'm beginning to see ..."

The ground rumbles. The soles of your feet vibrate. A zigzag line appears in the ground and the earth shifts.

"Cracks!" yells Klaus. "Quick. Get out! We don't want to be underground in an earthquake."

The pillars rock back and forth. Clouds of crumbling concrete fall from the ceiling. You scramble out after your boss, losing track of what happens to the elves. There's no time to worry about anyone but yourself. The stairs are falling away from beneath your feet. You grab the banister, feeling a splinter dig deep into your thumb. It hurts and starts bleeding, but you swallow your pain. Klaus reaches street level then turns and grabs your collar. You clutch your notebook as he flings you into his car. You land in the soft padding of Watson's back seat. He pants excitedly.

"Let's go," yells Klaus.

Watson doesn't have to be told twice. The crack

you saw in the cellar is spreading out into the street. Watson's wheels spin as he suddenly reverses, then performs a handbrake turn and sets off down the road. Your world is being torn to pieces. You've never seen anything like this. It reminds you of a disaster film. Shady Side residents are running about and screaming. Watson turns left, then right. He goes the wrong way around a roundabout. You can barely look. He takes a sharp turn that sends you rolling across the seat. You grab a seat belt but, before you can put it on, Watson slams on his brakes.

Klaus offers you a hand to pull you out of the footwell and pats the dashboard.

"Good boy, Watson," he says with an affectionate smile. "He's the best detective dog I ever had ... and look where he's brought us."

Feeling sick, you look up to see that you're outside the Haventry Exhibition Centre, where Enid is holding her Sinister Shindig and Moondance is running a meditation session. You're running out of time ... So which will it be?

? Do you want to go to the party?

Turn to page 178

PARTY CRASHING

? Or do you want to see the unicorn?

Turn to page 152

MOONDANCE'S EVENING MEDITATION

YOU AND KLAUS ARE BACK in the car. Klaus is feeding a bag of dog biscuits into the glove compartment. Watson munches happily as Klaus explains his plan to you.

"Before he was a car, Watson was a great detective dog. I first met him when he was working as a police dog for the UPF. He had the best nose in the business."

Watson beeps his horn.

"Sorry. He *has* the best nose in the business – which means as long as we have an item belonging to whoever we're tracking, he can find them."

You reach into your bag and pull out the dog lead

that the little girl dropped.

"I knew you'd have something," says Klaus, with a smile. He takes the lead and looks at it. "E... E... E... Enid the Evil Enchantress. Yes, this will do nicely."

He steps out of the car to hold it up to Watson's bonnet. As soon as he gets the scent, Watson begins to rev his engine. Klaus is only just back inside the car when Watson's wheels spin and he heads off.

Klaus tries to steer the car straight, but Watson is on the trail of the scent now. He will doggedly follow it, even if that means driving

through shopping centres,

down escalators

and across back gardens.

You wave apologetically at the confused pedestrians as you make your way across town. You're relieved when you finally come to a screeching halt outside a laundrette called Wash Like an Egyptian.

"Is she in here?" says Klaus.

Watson bounces up and down on his suspension in response, making you feel seasick. You open the door and jump out. Klaus does the same.

"Wait here," he says to Watson. "We may need a quick getaway. Remember, if this is Enid, she is not to be trifled with. And if she has the magic, she could literally turn us all into trifles."

Klaus chuckles but you're not so sure it's funny. You step inside the laundrette to see two mummies folding sheets. It's hard to tell where the mummies end and the sheets begin.

Neither of them pays you the slightest bit of attention, but the little girl with a basket on her lap looks up at you and smiles sweetly.

"Enid the Evil Enchantress, I presume," says Klaus.

"Never heard of her. I'm jutht a thweet little girl called, er ... Thynthia?"

"Save it and drop the lisp," snaps Klaus. "I know it's you. Watson just led us straight here."

"Watson? Oh, how is he?" The little girl's

manner changes as she peers over your shoulder and gives Watson a little wave through the window. "It's such a shame about Susan turning him into a car. Mind you, I heard she ended up as a caravan."

"We haven't got time for this," says Klaus. "We need to get the dragon back to sl—"

He stops when he spots a puff of smoke drift up from the laundry basket. A head emerges from under a blanket. It belongs to the cutest dragon you've ever seen.

"Er, if this is Betty, then she's a lot smaller than we've been led to believe," says Klaus.

"Oh, no. This is Betty's great-grandson, Mr Snuggles."

"Ri-ght." Klaus looks thrown by this. "Why have you been pretending to be a little girl all day?"

"I was trying to avoid autograph hunters. They're the worst. That's the thing about being known as the most evil enchantress the world has ever known. Everyone wants a piece of me. Or people want to be turned into something. Or to be given scars in the shape of lightning – which I don't do by the way."

"You've been hiding from the authorities and from your own League of Evil all day just to avoid autograph hunters?"

"Well, no. Not just because of that," admits Enid. "I changed my form into this after the coffee morning, but when I went back to Folly Heights, I saw that Mr Snuggles had escaped. I was out looking for him when the magic vanished."

"Where did you look for him?" asks Klaus.

"My first thought was that he'd gone for a run around in Snark Park, but he wasn't there so I tried the secret meeting. He knows there's often cake at the meetings and Mr Snuggles does enjoy a lemon drizzle, don't you?" She wrinkles her nose affectionately at the dragon. "But he wasn't there either. Then I remembered how much he loves hiding in here. I think it's the warm towels."

"You're trying to tell me that the reason no one's seen you all day is because you were searching for your pet dragon?" says Klaus, clearly struggling to believe it.

"Why, Mr Snuggles isn't a pet – he's my familiar."

"But I thought Mr Evans was your familiar."

"I wish I'd never thwarted and enslaved him in the first place. He's so ungrateful. Operation Overthrow, indeed." She shakes her head. "Mr Snuggles will be a much better familiar once I've trained him up."

Klaus raises his eyebrows. "I can't see Mr Evans being happy about that."

"That's true," says Enid. "Mind you, I don't think it'll matter. I get the feeling that we're all about to meet Mr Snuggles's great-grandmother, and then no one's going to be happy. Well, apart from Mr Snuggles."

The shop rattles as another earthquake strikes, and

a chasm

splits open

across the

tiled floor.

A window suddenly shatters. You shield your eyes from the shards of glass.

"Quick. Get out!" urges Klaus.

You lose track of what happens to Enid as you try to escape the laundrette. One of the mummies slips into a crack, grabbing another's wrappings, causing him to spin round and unravel.

"The dragon is awake!" yells Klaus. "We need to—"

You miss his last words as the floor beneath your feet gives way and you slide into the gaping hole. A scream rings out. You suspect it came from your own throat. In amongst all the heat and terror, you hear a rumbling from below. It's the sound of a creature bigger and older than any you have ever encountered. The cry of something beyond your imagination.

As you fall, there's only one question going round your head: is this the end?

SQUI-DOMP!

You land on something soft and squidgy. You sit up and try to get your bearings, but you can't see a thing. Whatever you've landed on shifts to the side and you tumble over. Getting to your feet is like trying to stand on ice.

Then comes a sound as low and ominous as thunder. A red light flares up. You can't make out the source but it allows you to see that you've landed on a massive golden eye. An eyelid the size of a bedsheet closes, scooping you up and flicking you on to the brow of this vast creature.

The surface beneath your hands is as hard as rock but there are ridges: huge scales on the skin of a dragon so big that you just almost fell into its pupil.

"So you've met Betty, then?"

As your boss climbs over the top of the dragon's head, relief floods through you, but another low growl reminds you that the danger is still very real. Klaus grabs on to a jagged ear then slides down to join you.

"Betty is still trapped beneath tons of soil and rock," he says. "But it won't be long before she wriggles free."

The huge dragon opens her mouth, revealing rows of teeth as large as boulders. As she lowers her jaw further you see the tongue, as big and red as a bus.

"I have an idea of how to get out of here," says Klaus, "but you have to trust me."

You do trust Klaus. You follow him as he crawls

towards the dragon's huge, smoking snout. Klaus reaches into the gushing smoke and grabs hold of a hair that's sticking out of a nostril. He nods at you and you can tell he wants you to do the same. You aren't happy about it but you take hold of the huge nasal hair.

"Now pull."

You don't really understand but you look up and see a speck of light. It's the sky. You tug as hard as you can. Klaus is much stronger than you and clearly causes Betty some pain. She tilts her head back.

Klaus climbs on to the tip of her nose, then reaches down and helps you do the same. "Now we've got the angle, we just need a little push." He reaches in his pocket and pulls out a sachet of pepper. "You never know when you're going to need more seasoning. Brace yourself," he says.

You nod even though you have no idea how to go about this. Klaus tears open the sachet and drops it into the nostril.

"AH ..."

"Take my hand."

"AH ..."

Klaus throws his arms around you. There's a sudden explosion of noise and a rush of wind as the dragon sneezes.

Everything is a blur. The tickle of Klaus's arms, the rush of hot air as you fly up, propelled by the sneeze. The burning heat of the dragon's breath gives way to the fresh evening air. You land with a thud. Klaus cushions your fall. You are back above ground. There's a huge crater beside you. You peer over the edge into the dark cavern. A few seconds ago you were at the bottom, sitting on a dragon the size of a city.

"Where are we?" asks Klaus.

You're wondering the same thing. The laundrette is nowhere in sight. You've landed outside Shady Side Stadium where the opening ceremony is due to kick off shortly.

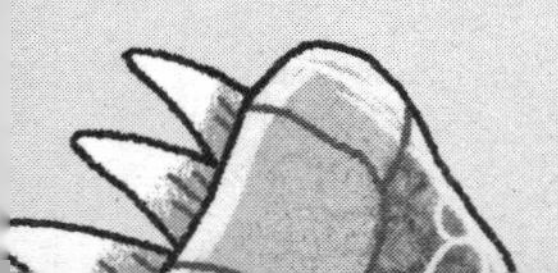

The whole stadium is shaking. There are legions of witches and wizards evacuating as fast as their legs can carry them. Some of them hop on to brooms, forgetting that the magic has vanished, then sheepishly run along on foot. You've never experienced anything like this before. Buildings that have stood for decades are crumbling along the street. You spot a couple of gargoyles clinging on to the side of one as it sways back and forth. Betty's thick black smoke billows out of the huge cracks that snake through the ground.

Through the chaos you see three familiar figures heading towards the stadium. Grand Master Dimbleby is hobbling as fast as his feet will carry him towards Door A. He's steadying himself with his staff and keeps looking over his shoulder.

Nigel Rigmarole is entering through Door C, protesting as the crowd coming the other way barge into him. He wears a crown and royal robes, and angrily waggles a long purple feather at the crowd.

The third person is shorter than Nigel and yet appears to be having no problem navigating her way through the crowd. Evil Enid, still in the form of a sweet little girl, is walking towards Door B. She's carrying the laundry basket. You wonder if all this chaos be the result of a fond owner who just wants to reunite her pet with his grandmother. It sounds incredible but, this being the Shady Side, you know nothing is impossible.

"Three suspects and we're almost out of time," says Klaus. "We have to follow one of them and we can't afford to make any mistakes now."

This has been an unusual case from the start. None of the suspects had an obvious reason for committing the crime and yet your gut tells you that one of these people will lead you to the answer. You pray that your instincts are right. It's down to you to solve the case, but which door will you choose? It's time to decide.

? Will you follow Grand Master Dimbleby through Door A?

Turn to page 203

A MUDDLE AND CONFUDDLE

? Or Enid the Evil Enchantress through Door B?

Turn to page 194

OPERATION OVERTHROW

? Or Nigel Rigmarole through Door C?

Turn to page 185

AN AMBITIOUS ELF

YOU'RE STANDING IN A CORRIDOR on the top floor of Haventry Exhibition Centre. You can hear the clink of glasses, muffled chatter, and the occasional maniacal laugh accompanied by a cry of "The world will be ours!" and "We shall smite them all!"

The Sinister Shindig for evil witches and wizards is in full swing. You recognize a few people inside, including Night Mayor Franklefink, who is chatting to Mr Evans, Enid's familiar. A waiter holds out a tray and they each take a glass. You want to hear what they're saying but you can't catch the words beneath the babbling of the partygoers.

You hear a toilet flush. A door opens and Klaus appears.

"Ah, hello," he says with a sheepish smile. "Sorry, but I've been drinking so much water to cool down and when you've gotta go, you've gotta go. Now let's check out this Sinister Shindig, shall we?"

The closer you get, the slower your feet move. Klaus pats you on the back and says, "I shouldn't worry. These evil folk talk a big game but they're mostly a bunch of pussy cats."

"I am neither big game nor a pussy cat," says a voice.

Standing in the doorway is a rather splendid-looking tiger in a bow tie. He speaks with a low, plummy voice.

"I'm terribly sorry. This is a private function." You notice that he's wearing a monocle.

"How much?" asks Klaus, pulling out his wallet.

"The very idea that I would take a bribe …!" says the tiger.

Klaus opens his wallet and pulls out a handful of notes.

"I've never been so offended."

Klaus pulls out another wad of notes.

The tiger looks shifty, then nods and whispers, "You have five minutes," before taking the money in his mouth and stepping aside.

As you cross the room, you hear the dark muttering of the evil partygoers. Some of them glance at you, but most are too busy scowling at Night Mayor Franklefink and Mr Evans. There are no windows in the room and it's extremely stuffy. Everyone is dressed in long, thick robes that are unsuitable for such intense heat. The smell of body odour is so strong that it reminds you of a time a wizard threw a stink spell at you. You can tell the heat

is bothering your boss too. Klaus pants like a dog as you make your way through the stuffy room. He mops the sweat from his brow with a wizard's tunic.

Franklefink is wagging his finger accusingly at the monkey. "If you know where she is, you need to tell me. And she'd better not be going back on our deal . . ."

"What deal would that be, then?" asks Klaus. "I assume you're talking about Enid."

"Enid the Evil Enchantress, actually," says Mr Evans. "Please use her full title."

"Stay out of this, Klaus," says Franklefink.

"The Night Mayor of Haventry is enjoying a drink at a party thrown by an evil witch who wants to destroy the world. I think this is every citizen's business." Klaus grabs a wizard's tunic and wipes his sweaty forehead with it. "What deal have you struck, Franklefink?"

"Nothing untoward, I assure you. Enid is scheduled to appear on stage with me at the opening ceremony but she hasn't been seen all day," replies Franklefink. "I fear she might be backing out."

"Why would she back out?" asks Klaus.

"Maybe because she has an image to maintain?" Mr Evans replies. "She is supposed to be the embodiment of evil."

"Regardless, we had an agreement," says Franklefink.

"Yes, and of course I understand," says Mr Evans. "I am her most loyal servant and would follow her to the ends of the earth but some of our less enlightened members ..." He lowers his voice to a whisper as he becomes aware that more people in the room are trying to listen in. "Some of them would sooner hand in their league badges than see their leader stand on stage with someone like you."

"It's her choice, not anyone else's." Franklefink jabs his finger angrily at the monkey. "And don't think word hasn't reached me about Operation Overthrow either."

Mr Evans laughs, raises his glass and says loudly, "Our intention to take over the world is hardly a secret and when we win the vote everyone will know."

A few witches in the corner cheer but most look distinctly unimpressed.

"You know very well that isn't what I'm talking about," snarls Franklefink.

The conversation is interrupted by a sudden tremor. The waiter's tray tips and several glasses crash to the ground, smashing into pieces.

"I think it's time you left." You feel something tickle your ears. You turn around to discover that the tiger is back. He bares his teeth and lets out a low growl.

"Don't get your whiskers in a twist," says Klaus. "It's too hot in here for me anyway." He turns to Franklefink and Mr Evans. "I'll see you two later."

"Yes, I look forward to seeing you both at the opening ceremony at Shady Side Stadium at ten o'clock," says Franklefink. "It's going to be a monstrously rewarding experience for everyone!"

As soon as you're out of the room, Klaus says, "Franklefink never gives you the whole truth, and that monkey knows more than he's letting on, but I've had an idea about how we can find Enid. Come on."

He marches towards the exit, but you pause to look at a poster with a picture of Moondance sitting cross-legged on a cloud. An arrow points towards a staircase. Below it, are the words:

Find Enlightenment This Way!

? If you haven't already been to the unicorn's meditation workshop, there's still time to go.

Turn to page 152
MOONDANCE'S EVENING MEDITATION

? Or you could find out what Klaus's idea is to find Enid?

Turn to page 166
WITCH-SNIFFER WATSON

AN AMBITIOUS ELF

Shady Side Stadium has played host to a range of extraordinary events over the years, from ogre wrestling to ghost tennis, but it's never held this level of danger and chaos before. You dart towards the entrance labelled *Door C* but a sea of pointy-hatted magical folk is rushing towards you. Everyone is screaming. The ground tremors are almost constant and flashes of fire leap from the cracks in the ground around you.

"Magical folk, please remain calm."

Night Mayor Franklefink's voice comes from the speakers, echoing around the huge auditorium. You push your way through the crowd but find yourself tangled up in robes. Panic sets in as you're dragged backwards, fearing you will be crushed in the stampede.

"I've got you."

Klaus's large, hairy hand tickles your neck as he plucks you up and out of the crowd until it passes. He puts you down. You feel shaken but determined. Nigel is in a glass lift heading up to the first floor.

"I see him too," says Klaus. "Let's take the stairs."

As you try to keep up, dodging chunks of plaster crashing down from the ceiling, you reflect on how so much detective work is about instincts. All day the name 'Rigmarole' has come up again and again. As you follow Nigel, your gut is telling you that this is the right path but you also know that there's more to be revealed. Your brain is alive with possibilities.

"Please don't panic. Everything is under control,"

says Franklefink's voice through the speaker.

The idea that Night Mayor Franklefink has everything under control would be laughable if it wasn't so terrifying. You reach the top of the stairs in time to see a door slam shut.

"The time for sneaking and spying is past," says Klaus. "Now we need to be accosting and accusing." He opens the door into a viewing room with plush chairs and a glass table filled with sumptuous nibbles. At the end of the room, Nigel and Sandra Rigmarole are standing by the balcony overlooking the empty arena. They're in the middle of an argument. Nigel is clutching his quill. Sandra is gripping a small, stripey pole.

"I supported you. All I'm asking is that you trust me now," says Sandra Rigmarole.

"Supported?" says Nigel. "You called me a silly old elf."

"I still came along to your coronation. It's not my fault that no one else did. What can I say? The monarchy simply isn't very popular with elves these days."

"As popular as garlic bread at a vampire dinner party," says the stripey pole in Sandra's hand.

"I've a good mind to snap that blasted opinion pole of yours in two," says Nigel. "I don't see why you have to take it everywhere you go!"

"It's vital that we keep tabs on how we're doing," says Sandra.

"I think you mean on how Franklefink is doing," says Klaus, announcing your presence.

Kevin and Sandra Rigmarole turn to look at you. From the tension in the room and the spark in your boss's eyes you can tell he's found the missing part of the puzzle. Sandra Rigmarole has been lurking at the fringes of this investigation. Now is her moment to step out into the spotlight.

"The opinion pole was never monitoring the *council's* popularity, was it? It's informing you how unpopular Franklefink is, isn't it?"

"As the elected Night Mayor, he must take responsibility for this mismanaged chaos," says Sandra.

"And how low does it have to get?" demands Klaus.

"I don't know what you mean by that," says Sandra but you notice Nigel looking at her with renewed suspicion.

"I think you do," says Klaus. "Franklefink's plan was to turn this opening ceremony – for an event that *you* organized – into a showcase for his new monster."

"That shows what you know. You think this is just about Enormelda?" scoffs Sandra, incredulously.

"Er, I did until you said that," says Klaus, glancing at you.

"Enormelda is a gimmick," says Sandra. "Something to draw the crowds. The real announcement is the unveiling of Everyday Monsters, his brand-new monster-making business."

"His what?"

Sandra points at the stage where Franklefink is making announcements into a microphone. Enormelda lies lifeless on a slab beside the Monster Maker. Behind her, hundreds of plain white boxes are stacked up.

"Every one of those contains a mini monster that will take care of all your domestic needs," says Sandra. "He even dragged my husband in to deal with repairs."

"He's barely paying me, but if I refuse, he'll get someone else to do it. And his monsters are designed to meet *all* your household needs. No one will need magical appliances any more. So I either sign up with him or I get run out business," moans Nigel.

"Yes, Franklefink is treating you very unfairly," says Sandra.

"Is that why you stole the magic?" asks Klaus.

Sandra glares at him, but makes no effort to respond.

"Ah, no, it wasn't just about protecting your husband," continues Klaus. "This is about bringing Franklefink down, isn't it?"

"That inept, self-centred man doesn't deserve to be Night Mayor," says Sandra angrily. "He thinks he can buy popularity by giving out free monsters?"

"As popular as a siren at a karaoke contest," squeaks the opinion pole.

Klaus continues. "But without magic, Franklefink's

plans would be ruined and his popularity would be at an all-time low ... allowing someone like you to swoop in and replace him at the next election."

Sandra lets out a short sharp laugh that fails to hide her annoyance. "Whether or not I decide to run for Night Mayor is irrelevant," she says. "I've only ever acted in the best interests of the community."

Another dramatic quake causes the room to shudder. Glasses rattle on the tables then fall, smashing on the floor. Cracks snake through the floor, walls and ceiling.

"Oh, my queen. What have you done?" Nigel places an arm around her.

Sandra doesn't deny it. Now that you're face to face with the thief, you understand her motives, but that doesn't justify the chaos and destruction this ambitious elf has wreaked upon your hometown.

There's one more thing you need to know. What did she use to steal the magic?

Through the speakers, you hear Franklefink's voice sounding increasingly panicked.

"Please remain calm.
Everything is under control.
Our magical technicians assure
me that they should have
the magic on shortly."

"As popular as a zombie at a—"

"Oh, be quiet," yells Sandra Rigmarole, angrily rattling the opinion pole. You spot a tiny spark fly from the top and suddenly understand what you need to do.

There's no time to lose. You leap forward and snatch the pole from Sandra's hands. As soon as your fingers close around it, you sense its incredible power. You close your eyes and wave the pole. You feel a sudden rush of fizzing energy that makes your fingers tingle. You speak.

"Cauldrons bubble, fires burn,
Now the magic must return."

There's a flash of light. You close your eyes, then open them and find that you're no longer in the stadium. You're standing in front of the abraca-router. Two fairies are there too.

"Is that the conductor?" asks Cabbage.

"Quick, put it in," says Moss.

You thrust the pole into the centre of the circle.

The huge ring hanging from the ceiling begins to move and you see a speck of light at its centre.

It grows larger and larger. You can feel tremors of power as the magic gushes from the pole to the circle. The light grows brighter – it spills out and wraps around you, drawing you inside the spinning ring.

To find out what happens turn to page 212
A KIND OF MAGIC

SHADY SIDE STADIUM HAS SEEN its fair share of extraordinary events, from ghoul races to zombie snooker, but now everyone is fleeing the shaking building as fast as their legs can carry them. Witches and wizards are running, crawling and hobbling for their lives as great chasms appear in the ground. Thick smoke gushes out, stinging your

eyes and making you choke and splutter. Several ghosts dressed in sportswear fly through the crumbling walls. You hear their words as they pass though you.

"I've haunted this stadium for fifty years, but I'm not sticking around for this," says a ghost who wears a yellow *Safety Officer* bib and has a javelin lodged in the side of his head.

"Yep. No more extra time to be had here," says a headless football referee.

Screams fill the air. You want to turn and run too but that's not an option. It's up to you and your boss to do something. You only hope it's not too late.

Night Mayor Franklefink's voice comes through the speakers.

"Magical folk, please remain calm."

Klaus leads the way as you reach the crowd. You follow in his wake, using him as a kind of giant, furry battering ram to get to Door B. Once inside, you search for Enid.

Since the moment you took this case, Evil Enid was the prime suspect. Everyone assumed it was her. She had the strongest motivation for causing all this chaos and destruction, but now you've met her, your view has changed. Life as a detective has taught you that you can't judge people by reputation. Enid is considered evil, but that doesn't quite match with your perception of her. Are you following her because you think she stole the magic or because you hope she will lead you to the answer?

"Please don't panic. Everything is under control."

Franklefink's voice is piped through the speakers.

If the rapidly running people can hear him, they aren't listening. You push past the last of them and spot Enid disappearing through a door marked *BOILER ROOM*.

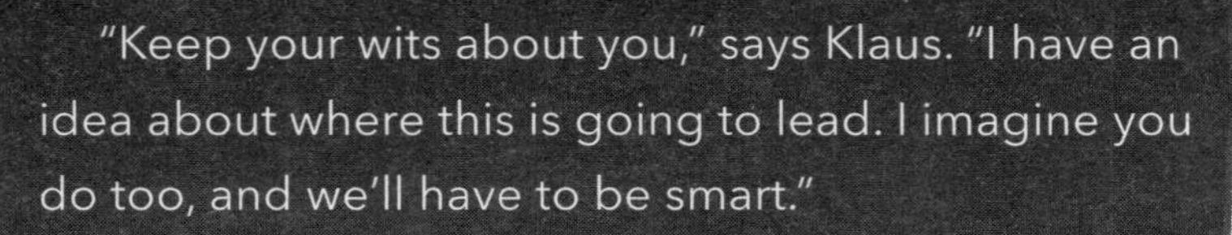

"Keep your wits about you," says Klaus. "I have an idea about where this is going to lead. I imagine you do too, and we'll have to be smart."

You reach the door and Klaus pushes it open. You follow him down the steps. Machinery chugs and groans loudly. These are the innards of the arena. You can no longer hear the sounds of panic from above and there's only flickering strip lighting and the red glow from the fires to see by. Mr Evans stands by a large metal wheel. Enid is in front of him, holding a laundry basket.

"There you are, you no-good, rotten primate," she says.

"Well, that's not very polite," replies Mr Evans.

"I know exactly what you're up to," says Enid. "This vent goes straight down to Betty's mouth. Her snores heat this entire stadium. Usually this is where they pour the sleeping potion, but you want her wide awake, don't you? You're waiting here to greet her."

"So what if I am? I'd rather ride to victory on the back of a real dragon than carry a baby one around in a basket like it's a doll."

Mr Snuggles sticks his head out from under the blanket and lets out a puff of smoke.

"Jealousy is an ugly emotion," says Klaus. "But I suppose you are being replaced so it's understandable."

Enid turns to face you. "Oh, you're back, are you? And you've brought *your* pet." She's referring to you.

"I think I see what's happening now. Just as Operation Overthrow looked like it was finally going to go ahead, Enid was replacing her faithful familiar with another," says Klaus.

"Faithful? Ha!" cries Enid. "And never mind me replacing him. He's trying to replace me!"

Klaus claps his hands together. "Oh, now I get it. Operation Overthrow was never about the ultimate war of good and evil. It refers to Mr Evans' plan to overthrow Enid."

"So what if it does?" says Mr Evans, scowling at the baby dragon. "She deserves to be overthrown."

"You wicked monkey," mutters Enid.

"The fact that you consider that an insult is precisely the problem," says Mr Evans. "Go on, tell them the truth. You're no longer the wickedest witch in the west, are you?"

"Really?" You and Klaus exchange a look, both of you wondering how much of this the other had already worked out.

Enid shrugs. "People change."

"When we met, I was the good one," says Mr Evans. "You convinced me of the ways of evil and now *you've* U-turned and gone good. Once, you were intent on setting the world on fire and watching it burn. These days, you'd rather make a nice cup of tea and watch telly. Or spend all your time playing catch with a baby dragon instead of rousing your League of Evil to rise up! Well, if you can't be the most evil leader in the world then I can." Mr Evans bangs his walking stick on the ground in anger, causing sparks to fly.

"Why didn't you tell us this at the laundrette, Enid?" asks Klaus.

"I didn't want the news to leak out before I announced it at the vote this weekend," she replies. "Then, after speaking to you about the theft, I put two and two together and realized it must be my jealous little familiar here who stole the magic."

"So, an evil witch who's lost interest in being evil," says Klaus, "and a familiar who wants to take over her evil empire."

"It's her fault. And his," says Mr Evans, pointing angrily at the dragon in the basket. "We're supposed to be voting to destroy the world this weekend. Instead, little miss goody two shoes will announce that she's seen the light. Can you even imagine how much damage that will do to the good cause of being evil?"

"It just seems like the world is intent on destroying itself without our help," says Enid. "So why not enjoy it while it's still here?"

Klaus turns to Mr Evans. "And so, angry at your boss's change of heart, you decided to steal the magic and create all this chaos, reminding the Evil League why they should vote for the uprising."

"Isn't it glorious?" Mr Evans beams with pride.

"And you got me out of the way by leaving the apartment window open so that poor Mr Snuggles escaped," says Enid, nuzzling her baby dragon.

"And while Enid went out to find her new familiar, her old one was planning to usurp her as supreme wizard of evil," says Klaus.

"Yes. Any second now, Betty will be free and I will ride upon her back and bring about a brand-new dawn of evil!" cries Mr Evans triumphantly.

You hear an announcement from the speakers on the level above. "Please remain calm. Everything is under control. Our magical technicians assure me the magic will be back on shortly."

"That ridiculous man," rants Mr Evans. "And to think you were going to stand on stage with him and agree to work with him. He's incompetent and corrupt but you're worse than that. You're ... you're ... you're nice."

"I no longer recognize that as an insult," says Enid.

"And as for this pathetic new pet of yours—"

The baby dragon screeches and sends a jet of fire at Mr Evans, causing him to cry out and drop his walking stick. It's only for a second but it's long enough for you to do what needs to be done.

You reach out and grab the stick. When your fingers wrap around it, you feel a tingle of power. The ground is shaking. Time is running out. You've never held a magical conductor before but you somehow know what to do. You wave the stick and cry:

**"Cauldrons bubble, fires burn,
Now the magic must return."**

Sparks fly. With a *WHOOSH*, the magic transports you away from the boiler room and to the golden ring of the abraca-router, with Cabbage and Moss now either side of you.

"That's it! You've got it!" says Moss.

"Now stick it in the abraca-router and it will release the magic," says Cabbage.

The idea of handling so much power terrifies you. It feels like someone has just asked you to stick your fingers into a high-voltage plug point. You're not sure if you'll survive but you also know that this is no time to quibble. You close your eyes and thrust the stick into the circle.

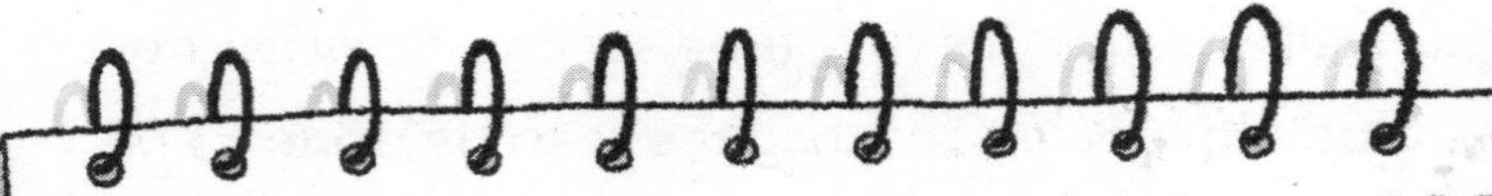

? To find out what happens turn to page 212
A KIND OF MAGIC

A MUDDLE AND CONFUDDLE

SHADY SIDE STADIUM HAS SEEN its fair share of nail-biting moments – from penalty shoot-outs in the five-a-side Phantom Football final to the photo finish in the mermaid backstroke – but nothing like this. You follow Grand Master Dimbleby as he hurries towards Door A, but all the other magical folk are moving in the opposite direction. Many of them are screaming as the ground pulls away from beneath their feet. The smoke that gushes out of the stadium fills your lungs. You hear the thundering approach of hooves and dive out of the way to avoid being trampled by a stampede of centaurs. With everyone leaving in such a hurry, you wonder if running towards this building is really a good idea, but you've made your decision.

As Head of the Magic Circle, Grand Master Dimbleby is responsible for looking after the town's magic but could he also be responsible for its disappearance? Running behind Klaus, you push your way through the crowd and into the building where you can hear an announcement coming through the speakers.

"Please remain calm," says Night Mayor Franklefink.

You glimpse Dimbleby's long robe disappearing through a door that slams shut behind him. The sign on it reads:

Klaus has never been one to follow rules. He yanks open the door and you run in. Usually, you would follow your boss. This time, you take the lead. You follow a twisting corridor that brings you out on the back of the stage. You pause to catch your breath as you look out at rows and rows of empty seats in the vast stadium. Night Mayor Franklefink stands at a microphone in the centre of the stage. Grand Master Dimbleby is just ahead of you. To the left you spot a large, lifeless monstrosity. Enormelda lies on a slab next to the Monster Maker. Behind her is a pile of plain white boxes.

"Please don't panic. Everything is under control." When Night Mayor Franklefink speaks into the microphone you hear his amplified voice echo around the stadium.

"Under control?" says Grand Master Dimbleby. "A huge dragon is about to wake up and destroy the city, you utter foot … I mean, fool."

Franklefink spins around to face him. "I'm sure everything will be resolved very soon. I have absolute faith in—"

"Enough," cries Dimbleby. "Betty is rising. Without the magic, we are helpless to stop her. You should be excavating. No, what's the word?"

"Evacuating," says Klaus.

"That's the one," says Dimbleby.

"I have full confidence that—" says Franklefink.

"Confidence?" says Klaus. "Or arrogance?"

"Precisely." Grand Master Dimbleby nods vigorously. "He's so wrapped up in this ludicrous plan of his to fill the town with monsters, he doesn't care what's going wrong." The wizard's eyes light up. "I say, I got to the end of that without saying the wrong worms … Oh."

"Er, what? Did you say fill Haventry with monsters?" says Klaus.

You wonder what this means too. You pick up one of the white boxes, lift the lid and look inside to see a doll-sized monster, with stitches across its face and neck. It looks a bit like a monster toddler. It's one of the creepiest things you've ever seen and, working in this job, you've seen your fair share of creepy things. You're just glad it isn't moving.

"Put that back," says Franklefink.

Klaus lifts it out of the box to examine it. "What is this thing?"

"An Everyday Monster," says Franklefink. "My lifelong dream realized. A monster in every home in the Shady Side community. They'll take care of all your household needs. They're going to revolutionize this city. And one day … the world!"

Klaus holds it up by one leg and waggles it. "They're a bit on the small side."

"That's the beauty of them," says Franklefink. "They're the perfect size to do all your household chores, without getting in the way. They don't require food or warmth. They are designed to do precisely what they are told. They'll revolutionize this community."

"You mad scientists never learn, do you?" Klaus shakes his head. "But how is any of this connected with the missing magic?"

"It isn't. He's only ever cared about getting the magic back for launching his new product. He doesn't care about who took it."

These words are spoken by a new voice. Moondance materializes in the middle of the stage in a flurry of sparkles and twisting rainbows.

"What are you doing here?" says Grand Master Dimbleby.

"I'm here to do what I should have done hours ago: accost the thief, restore the magic and save the day," replies Moondance.

"What thief?" says Dimbleby.

"Why, you, of course," says Moondance.

"Me? Why would I steal the magpies … er,

magic?" protests Dimbleby.

"Oh, you poor confused soul," says Moondance. "You probably didn't know what you were doing, but it's perfectly clear to everyone that you've lost your marbles."

"How dare you! I know exactly where my marmalade is," replies Dimbleby.

Klaus slaps his forehead and gasps. "Of course. That's it." He glances at you and winks. "I was just trying to remember who first brought up the idea that the magic could have been taken by accident. It was you, Moondance, when we were back in the abraca-router room."

"So what if it was?" Moondance trots across the stage and gives his mane a defiant swish.

Klaus continues. "Everyone else felt sure that it was a theft, but you wanted to plant the seed of the idea that someone could have done this by accident."

"Which actually isn't very lively … er, I mean likely," says Dimbleby. "I'm sorry. I don't know what's wrong with me."

"Whereas I think I do," says Klaus. "Back at the Magic Circle headquarters, Moondance performed magic on the candle but there was more to that spell, wasn't there?"

"I have no idea what you mean," says Moondance, swishing his tail and letting out a small, nervous whinny.

Dimbleby gasps. "*That's* when I started getting words mixed up. You cast a … a … what's it called?"

"A confuddle spell," says Klaus.

Suddenly you're transported to the moment you first entered the chambers of the Magic Circle, and you remember how Moondance tapped Dimbleby's hand, sending sparks flying and propelling the candle into the air.

"Oh, come on, you've been getting confused for longer than that." Moondance addresses Grand Master Dimbleby. "There's no shame in admitting that you're no longer fit to do your job. And then someone more capable can step in."

"You mean someone like you?" says Klaus.

"If my fans begged me to step up and become Head of the Magic Circle, it would be churlish to let them down," admits Moondance.

"But … but … but … what?" stammers Dimbleby. "You mean the whole thing was just a plot to replace me as Head of the Magic Circle?"

"It does sound a bit on the extreme side," says

Franklefink. "Not to mention inconvenient for the rest of us."

Moondance stomps his feet and scowls. "Inconvenient?" he says, with a dismissive neigh. "Don't you see? This isn't just about getting rid of Dimbleby. It's about wiping the slate clean – the dawn of a new future in which magic is shared with everyone."

"Er, and by wiping the slate clean you mean wiping this city off the face of the earth and making sure that everyone in the world becomes aware of dragons and magic, and ... well, all of us?" says Klaus.

"Yes! From this fiery beginning we could build a world held together by the strongest magic of all ... love," says Moondance with a wistful smile.

"So you were planning on allowing Betty to rise?" says Klaus.

"I still am," retorts Moondance. "You're here telling me your theories, but any minute now it won't matter because it will be too late. The future will be upon us. The slate will be clean!"

You don't hesitate. You know what to do. You reach up and grab Moondance's horn. As soon as your hands close around it, you sense its magic surge through you. In a loud, clear voice, you cry:

**"Cauldrons bubble, fires burn,
Now the magic must return."**

The unicorn horn pulsates with magical power. To your surprise, you understand how to harness it. You concentrate on what needs to happen. In the blink of an eye you are no longer onstage with the others. You're standing in front of the abraca-router. The fairies, Moss and Cabbage, are by your side.

"That's it," says Moss. "You've found the magical conductor!"

"Now stop messing around and bring the power back," says Cabbage.

The horn is still attached to the unicorn but it's in your hands – you have the power to do what needs to be done. You push the horn into the centre of the abraca-router. You see the huge ring begin to move and feel a wave of magic rush over you, blasting you backwards.

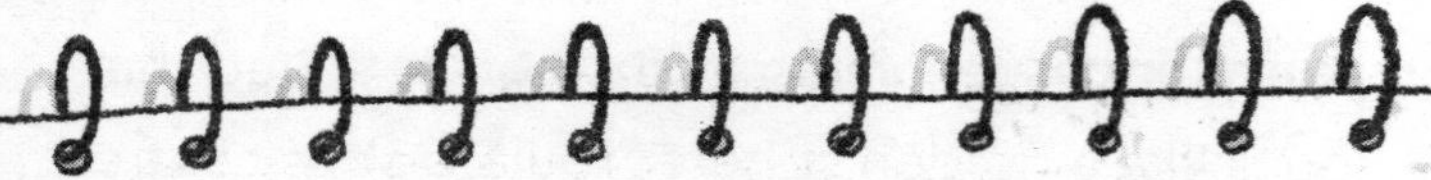

? To find out what happens turn to page 212
A KIND OF MAGIC

"ARE YOU FEELING OK?" SAYS a voice.

"I shouldn't imagine so, Cabbage. This human has just acted as a conductor for a hundred thousand giga-whizzes of magic. There's a good chance that they won't survive at all."

"It's all right, Moss. I can see some movement. Look! The eyes are opening now. Hello."

Your eyelids peel away to reveal the two fairies, buzzing around the room. Apart from them, nothing is clear. Is the room spinning or are you? The magical ring is revolving at such great speed that it looks like a golden sphere. You are at its centre – sitting in a chair. The impossibility of this fact makes your brain ache.

"I'm glad you're still with us," says Cabbage. "You saved the city. You and your yeti boss, that is."

"Yes," says Moss. "Luckily, as soon as you grabbed the conductor and spoke the words, the stolen magic gushed back into the abraca-router."

"And gushed through you," says Cabbage.

"Yes, about that …" says Moss.

"What?" asks Cabbage.

"I have a theory I'd like to share, if you'd like to hear it."

"I'd love to hear it." Cabbage comes to rest on your shoulder, sitting down and crossing his legs.

Moss lands on your other shoulder. "A hundred thousand giga-whizzes of magic is a lot to travel through a human body."

"It's a lot to travel through anyone's body."

"Agreed. It's not unlikely that a human who had just conducted that much magical power might be left with some after-effects."

"What a fascinating theory. Such as?"

"I wouldn't be surprised if they ended up a bit magic themselves," says Moss.

You stretch out your fingers and wiggle your thumb, surprising the fairies almost as much as yourself when tiny sparks fly from your fingertips.

Out of nowhere, two floating heads appear. They're the witches, Bridget and Burnella Milkbird.

"Well, how about that? Hello, you two," says Cabbage. "I trust all is well with the sleeping potion?"

"Yes, we made a fresh batch right away and Betty is back to the land of nod thanks to us," says Bridget.

"Thanks to you," says Burnella, looking deep into your eyes. "How does it feel to be the hero, then? Gone to your head, has it?"

You would answer, but all this spinning and twirling is making you dizzy. Your legs feel as heavy as lead but your arms are as light as feathers. You clap your hands together, creating a splash of fireworks.

"How did you do that?" demands Bridget.

"You have powers now too, eh?" says Burnella.

You look down at your hands and, for a fleeting moment, you feel as though you're holding a book.

You imagine that this is a story you're reading rather than a life you're living. But no. This is real. You can perform magic – and you've solved the mystery.

"I knew this one was special," says Burnella.

"Oh, you always say that," replies Bridget.

But you know what she means. You walk on the Shady Side of town because you feel at home here. Now that you're brimming with magical energy, you truly belong.

"You're wondering if things could have been different, aren't you?" says Burnella. "You have the power to go back and see. So what do you want to do next?"

? Do you want to go back to the beginning of the case and find a different way through?

Turn to page 9

MAGICON

? Or will you go back to the last time you saw the witches in the office?

Turn to page 129

THE BETTY PROBLEM

? Or will you find a whole new case to work on?

Look out for THE TRANSYLVANIAN EXPRESS

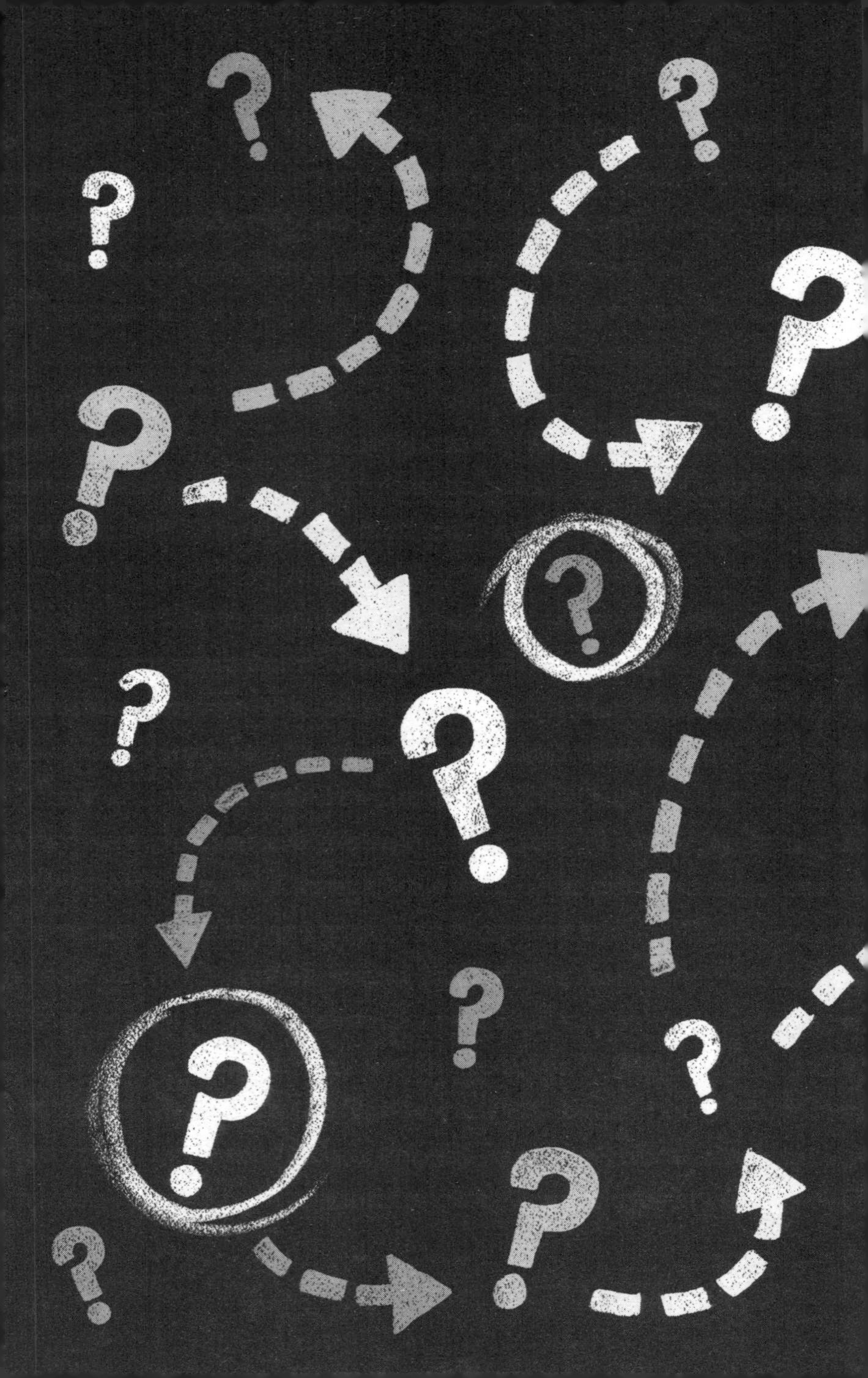

ALSO AVAILABLE

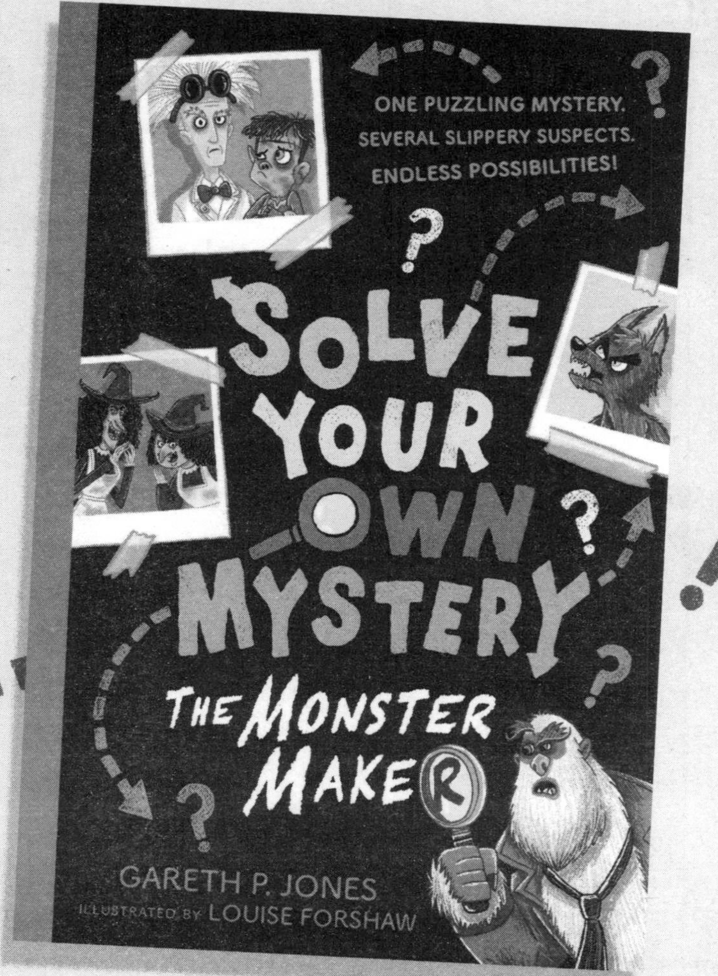

ALSO AVAILABLE

ABOUT THE AUTHOR

GARETH P. JONES is the Blue Peter Award-winning author of over forty-five books for children of all ages, including *The Thornthwaite Inheritance*, *The Considine Curse* and *Death or Ice Cream*. His series fiction includes Ninja Meerkats, Adventures of the Steampunk Pirates, Pet Defenders and Dragon Detective.

Gareth regularly visits schools all over the world as well as performing at festivals. He writes songs for all his books and has recently written a musical about a long-eared rabbit. He lives in south-east London with his wife and two children.

ABOUT THE ILLUSTRATOR

LOUISE FORSHAW is an illustrator from the north east, living just outside Newcastle upon Tyne.

She lives with her fiancé and three noisy Jack Russell Terriers: Lilah, Piper and Bandit.

To date, Louise has illustrated over seventy children's books. When she isn't drawing yeti detectives or being barked at by her dogs, she loves reading lots of books and binge- watching TV shows about vampires.

SOLVE YOUR OWN MYSTERY

The Transylvanian Express ?